Ben had not intended to get involved with Gwen.

But she was alone and a million and ten things could happen to her and no one would be around to even discover her, let alone rescue her. So if Ben made himself her protector for the next few months, he wasn't doing anything but being a good neighbor. Besides, he was her landlord. He had a responsibility to make sure she was safe while she was on his property.

He just couldn't get too attached to her, which would be the tricky part if he had to spend too much time watching her smile, listening to her soft voice, and enjoying the very fact—so clearly demonstrated by her pregnancy—that she was a woman.

* * * * *

Dear Reader,

Silhouette's 20th anniversary celebration continues this month in Romance, with more not-to-be-missed novels that take you on the romantic journey from courtship to commitment.

First we revisit STORKVILLE, USA, where a jaded Native American rancher seems interested in *His Expectant Neighbor*. Don't miss this second book in the series by Susan Meier! Next, *New York Times* bestselling author Kasey Michaels returns to the lineup, launching her new miniseries, THE CHANDLERS REQUEST.... One bride, *two* grooms—who will end up *Marrying Maddy*? In *Daddy in Dress Blues* by Cathie Linz, a Marine embarks on his most terrifying mission— fatherhood!—with the help of a pretty preschool teacher.

Then Valerie Parv whisks us to a faraway kingdom as THE CARRAMER CROWN continues. *The Princess's Proposal* puts the lovely Adrienne and her American nemesis on a collision course with...love. The ever-delightful Terry Essig tells the tale of a bachelor, his orphaned brood and the woman who sparks *A Gleam in His Eye*. Shhh.... We can't give anything away, but you *must* learn *The Librarian's Secret Wish*. Carol Grace knows...and she's anxious to tell you!

Next month, look for another installment of STORKVILLE, USA, and THE CHANDLERS REQUEST...from *New York Times* bestselling author Kasey Michaels. Plus, Donna Clayton launches her newest miniseries, SINGLE DOCTOR DADS!

Happy Reading!

Mary-Theresa Hussey

Mary-Theresa Hussey
Senior Editor

Please address questions and book requests to:
Silhouette Reader Service
U.S.: 3010 Walden Ave., P.O. Box 1325, Buffalo, NY 14269
Canadian: P.O. Box 609, Fort Erie, Ont. L2A 5X3

His
Expectant Neighbor

SUSAN MEIER

Silhouette
ROMANCE™
Published by Silhouette Books
America's Publisher of Contemporary Romance

Special thanks and acknowledgment are given to Susan Meier for her contribution to the Storkville, USA series.

SILHOUETTE BOOKS

ISBN 0-373-19468-4

HIS EXPECTANT NEIGHBOR

Visit Silhouette at www.eHarlequin.com

Printed in U.S.A.

Books by Susan Meier

Silhouette Romance

Stand-in Mom #1022
Temporarily Hers #1109
Wife in Training #1184
Merry Christmas, Daddy #1192
*In Care of the Sheriff #1283
*Guess What? We're Married! #1338
Husband From 9 to 5 #1354
*The Rancher and the Heiress #1374
†The Baby Bequest #1420
†Bringing Up Babies #1427
†Oh, Babies! #1433
His Expectant Neighbor #1468

*Texas Family Ties
†Brewster Baby Boom

Silhouette Desire

Take the Risk #567

SUSAN MEIER

has written category romances for Silhouette Romance
and Silhouette Desire. A full-time writer, Susan has also
been an employee of a major defense contractor, a
columnist for a small newspaper and a division manager of a charitable organization. But her greatest joy in
life has always been her children, who constantly
surprise and amaze her. Married for twenty years to her
wonderful, understanding and gorgeous husband,
Michael, Susan cherishes her role as a mother, wife,
sister and friend, believing them to be life's real
treasures. She not only cherishes those roles as gifts, she
tries to convey the beauty and importance of loving
relationships in her books.

STORKVILLE, USA

Storkville folks hardly remember the day the town bore another name—because the residents keep bearing bundles of joy! No longer known for its safe neighborhoods and idyllic landscape, Storkville is baby-bootie capital of the world! We even have a legend for the explosion of "uplets"— "When the stork visits, he bestows many bouncing bundles on those whose love is boundless!" Of course, some—Gertie Anderson—still insist a certain lemonade recipe, which is "guaranteed" to help along prospective mothers, is the real stork! But whether the little darlings come from the cabbage patch or the delivery room, Storkville folks never underestimate the beauty of holding a child—or the enchantment of first love and the wonder of second chance....

Chapter One

"Aw, damn!" Sioux rancher Ben Crowe brought his truck to a screeching halt on the old dirt road that led to his home. He shoved open the door and jumped out, nine-year-old Nathan Eastman on his heels. "I knew something like this was going to happen!"

Ben was a tall man, at least six foot. When he reached very pregnant Gwenyth Parker, who was dragging a huge box up the steps of the cottage he'd rented to her only two days before, he towered over her. "What in the hell do you think you're doing?"

Because he was angry, and his voice dripped with it, he was surprised when she looked up and smiled. "I bought a walker for the baby," she said simply, her hazel eyes sparkling with joy.

Ben had heard all about the glow of pregnant women, but he had to admit this was the first time he'd actually seen it. Her eyes were so bright and her face was so radiant she could have lit the darkest night.

"No kidding," Ben said, then scooped the unwieldy

cardboard box out of her arms and carried it up the steps. "Don't you know you're not supposed to be lifting heavy things?"

"It's not heavy," Gwen replied, her smile in place, her beautiful blond hair reflecting the rays of the early September sun. "Who's your friend?"

"That's Nathan," Ben said, unlocking her front door because as her landlord he had a key. "Don't change the subject. I rented this property to you on the condition that you'd be a good tenant."

"I am a good tenant," she said, right behind him as he set the big box on the floor beside her kitchen table. When he turned around, she was directly in front of him.

Dressed in simple jeans, maternity T-shirt and a bright blue sweater coat that wasn't designed for a woman in her seventh month and didn't button over her tummy, with her wind-blown, shoulder-length hair tucked behind her ears, Gwenyth Parker was still impossibly beautiful, and Ben realized he could have stared at her lovely face all day.

It had been a long time since a woman stirred his senses. Because Gwen did, he took a step back, then shifted around her to go outside.

"Are there any more boxes in your car?"

She shrugged. "A few. But really, Mr. Crowe, I didn't buy anything I couldn't carry myself."

He grunted an unintelligible response to that, then hurried out the door and down the steps to her car.

He didn't know much about the newest resident of Storkville, Nebraska, except that she was pregnant and she had divorced her husband, the baby's father, before she moved here. That was the first reason he'd been reluctant to rent the roadside cottage to her. He couldn't understand or condone a woman raising a baby alone when she had a perfectly good husband. The second reason was that he was afraid he would somehow become responsible for her. She had assured him he wouldn't, but in less than a week he was already carrying boxes.

"Where do you want these?" he asked, stepping into the kitchen again.

She pointed to the sofa in the small living room off to the right. "In there is good."

He gave her a patient look. "And how do you plan to get these up the stairs?"

Ben saw her pause, taking note of dark-haired Nathan, who still wore his good jeans and T-shirt from school and was behind Ben, more or less peeking around his waist at Gwen.

"Nathan," she said, "why don't you go out to the car and make sure there aren't any packages left?"

From the formal tone of her voice, Ben could tell her good mood was gone. Nathan must have sensed it, too, because he didn't say anything, only grinned and nodded, then darted out of the house.

"Look, Mr. Crowe," she said coolly, her once-smiling face now drawn in anger. "I'm pregnant, not sick. I'm perfectly capable of taking care of myself."

"I'm sure you are," Ben agreed, not quite understanding how a sweet disposition could go sour in the blink of an eye, but glad to have her mention the issue that troubled him about her. Since she brought up this subject, he felt permitted to pursue it. "Is that why you left your husband? To prove you could take care of yourself? Because if it is, you should be ashamed of yourself. Babies need two parents."

He hadn't expected her angry face to fall in dismay, but it did. He'd driven her from unreasonably happy, to angry, to sad so rapidly Ben immediately knew dealing with pregnant women wasn't his forte. He also knew he'd made a big mistake.

Quiet, stricken, Gwen said, "I think babies need two parents, too, but it wasn't my decision to get a divorce. It was my ex-husband's. If the choice had been mine, I would have raised my child with its father." With that she walked to the door. "If you don't mind, I have to put all this stuff away," she said, more than hinting that Ben should leave.

Confused because he was now more curious about her than before, but equally embarrassed because he'd upset her, he ran his hand across the back of his neck. Having been raised in foster homes, he understood his urge to confront her about not putting the welfare of her child first. But normally he had enough sense to stop himself from butting in if a problem wasn't any of his business. And since her marriage, her ex-husband and even this baby weren't any of his business, it puzzled him that he hadn't thought this the whole way through before he opened his big mouth.

"I'm sorry," he apologized contritely. "I didn't mean to be so blunt, but when it comes to kids I know I'm overly protective since my own parents abandoned me."

With a brief nod, she more or less conceded that she understood what he'd said, but Ben knew it was too late. Not only had he stuck his foot in his mouth, but he'd also hurt her.

Walking to his truck, he felt like a real idiot. A block-head, too stupid to tread lightly with a woman who had enough to deal with without having to listen to his criticism. He shouldn't have challenged her the way he had, but he quickly forgave himself because he truly was a person who cared about kids. Asking her that question, no matter how inappropriate, was second nature to him.

So that took care of forgiving himself. Now all he had to do was figure out how he could get *her* to forgive him.

Though he was a loner, who didn't really have a lot of contact with people and who definitely didn't care what people thought of him, Ben recognized this situation was different. He'd made a mistake, and he needed to fix it. But even before he reached his truck he knew that asking her forgiveness would be awkward and complicated and much more intimate than he intended to get with this woman. Which precluded making another apology, but, still, he wanted to do something. There had to be a way to make this up to her.

He opened his truck door and called to Nathan. "Come on, Nate. It's getting late and we've got to get going."

As Nathan almost tumbled down the steps of the cottage, having delivered the last of Gwen's packages, Ben realized that the perfect way to handle things without getting involved was right before his eyes. Because Nathan was too young to get a job and too energetic to stay in the house, his older foster parents encouraged him to leave the reservation and spend all his free time tagging along with Ben. Though Ben considered himself to be somewhat boring, particularly to a nine-year-old boy, Nathan never complained, confirming for Ben that he was incredibly lonely. Gwen needed someone, too, if only because she was by herself outside of town and no one would know if she got sick or hurt. She and the boy were a match made in heaven.

"Hey, Nate, how would you like to earn ten dollars a day?"

Climbing into the truck cab, Nathan turned his big brown eyes on Ben. "You know I would!"

Ben immediately reached into his wallet and pulled out a ten dollar bill. "All you have to do is stay with Mrs.

Parker, help with errands and make sure she doesn't do anything too difficult.''

"Today?" Nate asked, confused.

"Every day. Ten dollars a day, *every day*,'' Ben said, exaggerating the word so Nate would see the significance. "When I get home, I'll put this on the mantel in the den,'' he said, showing Nathan the ten dollars. "I'll put ten dollars on the mantel every time you spend the day with her. Then at the end of a week, if you go to her house five days, you'll have fifty dollars. But if you can go all seven days, spend a few hours after school every day and stop by on weekends, you'll have seventy dollars.''

From the way Nathan's eyes grew wide with every word Ben spoke, it was obvious he couldn't believe his good fortune. As if he wasn't going to miss this opportunity by reacting too slowly, the very second Ben was done making his proposition, Nathan yelped, "All right! Seventy bucks!'' then shoved open the truck door and scrambled out.

But Ben stopped him by catching his forearm. "You can't tell Mrs. Parker I'm paying you to stay with her and help her.''

Nathan blinked at him. "Why not?''

"She won't like that,'' Ben explained. "She's proud.''

"Oh,'' Nathan said, nodding his understanding.

"So tell her that you were curious about her and her baby and that's why you're back. We'll think up another story for tomorrow and the next day until eventually she'll just get used to having you around and she won't question you anymore.''

Recognizing that was what had happened when Nathan starting hanging around with Ben, Nathan grinned his agreement.

"But no matter what happens,'' Ben said, "you are not

to tell Mrs. Parker that I'm paying you to help her. In fact, don't tell her you're there to help at all. Just let her think you're curious about the baby and that you'd like to be her friend.''

Looking like a boy who was confident he could do this job, Nathan nodded, slammed the truck door and ran across the short front lawn to Gwen's porch.

Ben started his truck and quickly eased it onto the road, knowing it would ruin everything if Gwen saw him and that Nathan had enough common sense to return to the ranch if Gwen refused his offer. But he didn't think she would. He hadn't met a woman yet who didn't melt at Nathan's smile.

Driving home, Ben felt as if he was the smartest man on the face of the earth. If this worked, orphaned Nathan would be busy and happy, with a caring adult, as had been his foster parents' intent when they sent him to Ben, and Gwen would have company. In case she fell or became ill, Nathan would know to contact Ben. And Ben didn't have to feel guilty anymore. He was a genius.

Because Nathan didn't return to the ranch, for exactly one afternoon Ben felt he had the world by the tail. He was even whistling when he jogged up the porch steps of Gwen's cottage to retrieve Nathan and take him home, but when smiling Gwen opened her door to him and Ben felt an unexpected jolt of happiness seeing her, he started to reconsider everything.

''Hi,'' she greeted, obviously not holding a grudge for his mistake that afternoon.

''Hi,'' he said. An odd sense of something tingled through him. His first instinct was to think he was getting a crush on her, but that had to be wrong. Sure, Gwen was a beautiful woman. Actually, she was gorgeous. But she was also pregnant with another man's child. Now that he knew the real story, he had to suspect that Gwen hadn't yet had time to get over her ex—especially if she hadn't wanted the divorce.

Besides, he'd seen her often enough when he showed her the cottage and they negotiated her lease that if he were really getting a crush on her he would have felt it sooner, right? Right. If he were experiencing anything more than a reaction to her good looks, he would have felt it before this.

"I'm here for Nathan."

"Oh, yes," Gwen said, flustered. "I'm sorry."

"Don't be sorry," Ben said, stepping into her kitchen for the second time that day, but this time he noticed that her curtains were sunny yellow. She had a white lace tablecloth on the table and a bouquet of brown-eyed Susans. "I'm not in any hurry."

At that she turned. "Really? Because if you have time I made a casserole for dinner. There's plenty."

Ben grinned sheepishly. "I don't have that much time."

"Oh, I'm sorry," Gwen said, appearing flustered again.

Ben almost groaned at his stupidity. He knew he'd screwed up everything that afternoon by forgetting that pregnant women were emotional. Yet, he continued to hit all the wrong buttons with Gwen. Being too blunt. Speaking too soon. Not showing a little kindness.

"I'll just go upstairs and get him."

She turned to run up the steps, but Ben put his hand atop hers on the banister. Unfortunately, even though she stopped as he wanted her to, Ben also stopped. His heart stopped. His breathing stopped. And he was fairly certain all his brain cells stopped functioning.

The back of her hand was like satin. Smooth, warm satin.

Positive he must be getting sick or something, he cleared his throat. "Take your time," he said, and when his voice came out hoarse and whispery, he had to stifle a grimace.

What the hell was wrong with him?

Gwen disappeared up the steps, and as Ben waited for her return he oriented himself back to sanity. But when she walked down the stairs, the fading rays of the late-afternoon sun framed her in a yellow glow. Spontaneously, he wished he had a picture of her like that, and he knew sanity was nowhere around.

"Nathan was a very good boy today," she said, and Nathan beamed with pride.

"Well, that's good," Ben said, wanting only to get the heck out of this house before he said or did something else foolish. "When he said he was curious about you and the baby, I didn't think you would mind if he spent some time with you."

"Oh, I didn't," Gwen quickly said. "I loved the company."

"Good," Ben said.

Nathan tugged on his shirtsleeve. "She said I can come over anytime I want."

Ben risked a peek at her. "Is that so?"

Gwen shrugged and smiled. "I like the company."

That seemed to be all there was to say, but Ben didn't want to accidentally insult her again by jumping to the conclusion that the conversation was over if she didn't think it was, because he didn't want to feel any more responsible for her than he already felt. When he realized things had grown so quiet he could hear the tick of the clock, he also realized he'd been standing by her front door like an idiot for at least a minute. Almost as if he didn't want to leave.

"Well, Nate, let's go," he said, reaching for the doorknob. Nathan scrambled around him and wiggled his way between Ben and the opening. "He's got a lot of energy," Ben said, making excuses for Nathan's need to get outside. He certainly couldn't tell her the kid was anxious to get to Ben's home and see his ten dollars on the mantel.

"He does have a lot of energy," Gwen agreed with a laugh. "I can't tell you what a relief it was to have him around all afternoon. He did tons of little things for me. I didn't realize I had so many chores I was putting off until I could bend a little easier."

Though Ben would have happily scooted off her porch only three seconds before, for this he turned and faced her. He had no doubt Nathan would keep Gwen company, but he wanted to confirm Nathan was doing what he was being paid to do. "He *helped* you?"

"A great deal," Gwen assured Ben with a nod. "And he's a wonderful boy."

Her words were like a soothing balm, a confirmation for Ben that he'd really done right by her. No guessing. No assumptions. His smile was quick and genuine. "Yes, he is."

"I hope my child is as happy and energetic as he is."

Hearing the sweet, wishful, motherly tone of her voice, Ben realized why he suddenly felt differently around her than he had before. He'd lost his wall of protection. He'd already admitted to himself that Gwen was a beautiful woman. He'd admitted to himself that he found her attractive. But he'd always had the protection of thinking she must not be a good person to have yanked her child away from its natural father. Now that he had accepted that Gwen herself was abandoned, a good and decent person trying to do the best she could, it seemed his fortress against her appeal was gone. And all the rules had changed.

"Well, I'll see you around," he said gruffly, and bounded outside, not wasting another second.

Not only was he attracted to her, but with the knowledge that she was as blameless as she was beautiful, the door was open for him to pursue her...and he wanted to. That was what kept throwing off his concentration and his ability to reason. He really wanted to get to know her. She was pretty, sweet and delightfully charming. What man wouldn't want to spend time with her?

But there was one little problem.

He had no intention of settling down. None. Never. And a woman with a child on the way needed a commitment. Since Ben was not the kind of man who could make a commitment, he had to stay the hell away from her.

Chapter Two

Gwen didn't know why she hid her stash of shortbread cookies on the top shelf of her last cabinet behind the old dishes she never used. She didn't live with anyone, so no one would find her precious treat. And *she* knew where the darned cookies were. It wasn't as if she prevented herself from discovering them. She wasn't fooling anybody or accomplishing anything, only delaying the inevitable.

Thinking that her purpose must be to give herself time to change her mind about eating a hundred buttery calories for every cookie, she dragged a chair to the cupboards and climbed onto the seat. Then she took a minute to catch her breath because she was huffing and puffing from the slight exertion. Twenty pounds didn't seem like a lot, but when gained in seven months and distributed entirely to her middle, those twenty pounds had really thrown a monkey wrench into physical activity—not to mention her shape and mobility.

Since she wasn't concealing the cookies from intruders

and since she obviously wasn't deterring herself, she declared herself officially too clumsy to continue this little game at the same moment that someone knocked on her front door.

She groaned. Now she remembered why she hid these things. It was to keep them out of sight of visitors who would take one look at her bulging tummy and one look at the cookies and recognize she had absolutely no willpower.

"I'm coming," she called, when her guest knocked again. She lumbered off the chair and walked to her front door, realizing that in the city she might have worried about being so casual with unexpected visitors. But here in Storkville, Nebraska, she never gave callers a second thought. She hadn't met anyone who wasn't pleasant, and most people went out of their way to be kind and considerate...except for Ben Crowe, she thought with an involuntary sigh. When she had met the Sioux rancher she'd immediately thought he was the most handsome man in Cedar County, with his nearly black eyes and short, shiny black hair. But as they negotiated the deal for his cottage, it didn't take her long to realize he was also the most bossy, irritating chauvinist she'd come across in a long, long time. Every time she had contact with him his gruffness managed to confirm that opinion, but his behavior the day before had etched it in stone.

When she opened the door and saw Nathan, her bad mood disappeared. "Hey, Nathan!" she said, stooping down so they were eye level.

"Hi, Mrs. Parker," he said, his gaze dropping shyly.

"None of that Mrs. Parker stuff," Gwen said, then ruffled his smooth dark hair. "Didn't I tell you yesterday to call me Gwen?"

He nodded.

"Okay, then," she said, and attempted to rise, but couldn't. "Drat!"

"What's the matter?" Nathan asked, alarmed.

"Nothing," Gwen said. "I just need something to hold on to."

"Here," Nathan said, catching her arm. "I'll help."

Gwen knew Nathan's enthusiastic heart was in the right place, but she also knew his slight body could not support her weight. Still, not wanting to insult him, she allowed him to hold her left arm while she actually levered herself up by angling her right hand on the door frame.

"That's better," she said, then blew her breath out on a long sigh. "So how come you're here?"

He shrugged. "I don't got nowhere else to go. I got no parents. And you said yesterday I could visit anytime I wanted."

"That's right," Gwen said, directing Nathan to follow her into the kitchen, though she had the distinct impression she was being conned. She'd spent an entire afternoon with this kid yesterday and his grammar was perfectly fine. Now suddenly he was talking like a five-year-old.

"I live with foster parents on the reservation," he continued, as he sat on one of the captain's chairs by her round kitchen table. His dark hair was bright and shiny, but his dark eyes were dull with concern, as if he was afraid she didn't believe him. "They're nice, but they're old, and they don't like to play."

He'd told her as much the day before, but today there was an odd quality to his voice, almost a quiver. If he was duping her, it was only because he wanted company. Come to think of it, so did she. She was lonely. He was lonely. There was no harm in letting him hang around for a while. In fact, she decided to share her cookies with him and made her way over to the cupboard.

"Do your foster parents know where you are?" she asked as she climbed on the chair again.

He nodded. "I called from Ben's."

Ben's. Great. Did everything in this town revolve around Ben Crowe? "What did they say?"

"They said that I could come over as long as I didn't annoy you. And Ben said he'd pick me up later to take me back to the reservation."

That stopped her. She could see the surly rancher letting his little friend use the phone. She could even see him letting this boy follow on his heels because that might feed his ego. But to volunteer to go out of his way to take him back to the reservation? That made him seem almost—well, nice. "He did?"

"Yeah," Nathan said.

Hearing the obvious affection in Nathan's voice, Gwen turned around and looked down at him. "You really like that guy, don't you?"

"He's my friend."

The simple statement told Gwen many things, not the least of which was that Nathan didn't consider himself to have too many friends. Again, her opinion of Ben Crowe rose several notches.

Not wanting to go any further with this conversation, she put her attention on opening her cupboard door, but when she reached for the cookies, she felt off balance and stopped mid-stretch.

"What are you doing?" Nathan asked, sounding as if he felt she was crazy.

She cleared her throat. "Getting cookies."

"All right!" he said, apparently pleased at the prospect

of a snack. In two shakes, he was beside her chair. "Let me do this."

"Nathan, you're shorter than I am. If I can't reach them, you can't reach them," she protested, but before the words were completely out of her mouth, Nathan had hoisted himself onto the countertop. He swiveled around, shifted to his feet and had her cookies in his hand before she could make another sound.

"Here," he said, giving the cookies to her and jumping to the floor.

It wasn't the neatest way to go about it, and it certainly wasn't the most sanitary thing in the world to have someone stand on your countertop, but it worked.

"Thanks," she said, carefully getting off the chair. And it wasn't entirely safe for her to be climbing chairs anymore, either. Or carrying heavy packages, she conceded in her thoughts, though she still didn't like Ben's attitude when he stopped to help her the day before, because she wasn't an invalid. But she also had to admit that it had been good having Nathan here yesterday when she needed somebody to bend and stretch.

As she thought the last, an idea formed. She wasn't an invalid who couldn't do things for herself, but it certainly wouldn't hurt to have another person around the house to help her. At the same time, Nathan needed company, and he also was a nice little boy who could use a break from life.

"Nathan, how would you like to earn twenty dollars a week?"

His eyes widened comically and he gasped. "What?"

Proud of herself for coming up with such a good plan, Gwen smiled and sat at the table across from Nathan. "You saw how easily you got those cookies for me?"

He nodded.

"That showed me that I could really use some help around here. So, I'd be willing to pay you twenty dollars a week, if you would come over every day after school and just hang around in case I need something from a cupboard."

Big-eyed, Nathan said nothing, only licked his lips. Then he pulled his bottom lip between his teeth as if dismayed.

Baffled, Gwen wondered why he would hesitate to take her money, then she realized she might have insulted him. Or made him feel like a charity case. She hadn't been in Storkville long, but she knew the Sioux were a proud, strong people.

"I really need the help," she said, because she truly did. If his stay with her the day before hadn't proved it, her inability to reach those darned cookies had. She could lower everything to be within reaching distance, but what if she fell? When she chose to rent Ben Crowe's cottage on the edge of his property, she had gotten all the privacy she craved for both the baby and to be able to do her illustrations peacefully at home, but she had also isolated herself. With Nathan arriving every afternoon at three, she would at least know someone would find her if something happened.

More convinced than ever that she needed this child's assistance, Gwen said, "Please?"

He sighed.

"Pretty please?" she said, knowing he was weakening.

Nathan shook his head as if deliberating, though she couldn't think of a reason he would be reluctant to accept her offer. But suddenly he grinned broadly and tossed his hands in defeat. "Okay," he said, sounding unsure but committed.

Gwen said, "Great!" Each ate two cookies, then Gwen

sent Nathan on his first assignment. "There's a freezer in the basement," she said. "Would you please go down there and take out a package of hamburger?"

Nodding energetically, Nathan bounced off his chair and ran to her basement.

Gwen's chest puffed out with pride. Not only had she solved a problem for a sweet little boy, but she now had company for dinner. Unfortunately, because she felt she had to find some work for them to do to make Nathan feel his position was legitimate, she and Nathan got involved in organizing her closet and before she knew it it was after six o'clock. She wouldn't have glanced at the clock even then, except for the second time that day someone was knocking on her door.

"That's probably Ben," Nathan said authoritatively as he helped her maneuver herself out of the jumbled mess of clothes, shoes and boxes.

"Already?" Gwen said, dispirited. All afternoon she'd been looking forward to having company for dinner, and because she'd lost track of time she wouldn't have any. The disappointment that settled over her was acute and severe. Which caused her to realize she was much lonelier than she was letting everyone—even herself—believe and convinced her that she had made a very wise choice in hiring Nathan to be with her every afternoon.

But that didn't get her someone to share dinner with tonight.

"I told him I would call him when I wanted to go home, but he must have thought I forgot," Nathan said, following Gwen down the steps to her front door.

Expecting to see Ben, Gwen's mouth nonetheless fell open in surprise when she opened the door and he stood before her. Not because it was him, but because he looked absolutely magnificent. Dressed in a dark suit, complete with white shirt and raspberry-colored tie, Ben took her breath away. His short, neatly styled black hair accented a face that was all clean angles and smooth planes. His dark eyes pierced her with his usual no-nonsense stare. His munificent mouth never smiled.

"Hi," she said, then mentally chastised herself for the quiver in her voice. Yes, the man was attractive, but she was twenty-eight, not a schoolgirl. And he wasn't her type. After her disastrous marriage, Gwen had vowed to shift her choice of men from cool and demanding, to sweet and mellow. This guy was not mellow.

"Hi," he said distantly, his tone relaxing Gwen somewhat. Having reminded herself of what she wanted in a husband, she knew beyond a shadow of a doubt that she didn't have to worry about her attraction to this grumpy man. She wouldn't marry another difficult man on a lost bet.

"I'm here for Nathan."

"Actually, he's not ready yet," Gwen said, an idea forming in her head. "I promised him supper." She flashed Ben a winning smile. Her attraction to him no longer a consideration, she had no compunction about pulling out all the stops to retain her companionship for dinner. Besides, if she looked at this logically, all she was doing was being nice to her neighbor, her landlord. Certainly that couldn't hurt. "It's only hamburgers, but there's plenty if you'd like to join us."

She put her hand on Nathan's slender shoulder at the same time Nathan looked up at Ben and grinned. "Please," he said sweetly, and Gwen almost laughed. They couldn't have done that better if they'd rehearsed it.

From the expression on Ben's face Gwen could tell that he'd been all set to refuse her as he had the night before, until he looked down at Nathan's smile. The kid was good. Very good. No adult with an ounce of compassion could look at that angelic face and refuse him anything.

"All right," Ben said, but he sighed.

Gwen decided she couldn't even give him two minutes to debate this or he would change his mind. "Come on, Nathan, let's get the hamburgers on the grill."

"You can't grill. It's getting dark," Ben protested, but Gwen turned and smiled charmingly.

"It won't be dark for another hour, but the grill is on the deck and the deck has a light. If it gets dark, we'll turn it on." She smiled again. "Would you like a short-bread cookie while you wait?"

That seemed to confuse him. "Before dinner?" he asked incredulously.

Her smile became a grin. "I'm pregnant. I eat what I want, when I want. It's the only perk."

Though she thought he might have criticized her for that, Ben Crowe actually laughed, and a strange bubble of delight rose in Gwen's stomach. She told herself to ignore it, but it was hard not to be proud of yourself when you made such a surly man laugh. When he joined them in the kitchen and quietly, almost formally asked if he could assist with the dinner preparations, making him laugh again started to feel like a goal.

So she faced him and gave him her most genuine smile. "Do you like lettuce and tomato on your hamburger?"

He nodded. "Yes."

"Well, there's a tomato in the refrigerator and a head of lettuce. You could wash those," she said, then shifted her tone until it was serious, almost melodramatic. "But you would have to take off your jacket. Maybe even your tie."

It was the first time in her life Gwen had ever seen a man blush, and though she found his embarrassment endearing, it also puzzled her. Either he didn't know how to handle someone teasing him, or he was so unfamiliar with cooking that he didn't realize he needed to remove his coat.

"But Nathan and I can do that," she said quickly, hoping to make up for embarrassing him so he wouldn't get uncomfortable and change his mind about staying.

He shook his head and shrugged out of the black suit coat. "I'll do it," he said firmly.

Gwen decided to let the subject drop and went out to the deck to check on the hamburgers. "How's it going out here?" she asked Nathan.

Spatula in hand, he grinned up at her. "Really good."

Seeing how happy he was, Gwen ruffled his hair. "We should make a standing arrangement that you'll eat dinner with me every day so that I'll have help with the dishes."

Nathan nodded.

Gwen felt her bubble of excitement again, then Ben appeared at the sliding glass door leading to the deck. With his jacket gone and the sleeves of his white shirt rolled to his elbows, he added a dimension to his good looks that Gwen had all but forgotten existed. Sex appeal. Her merry bubble of excitement instantly transformed into a shiver of awareness.

"You cold?" Nathan asked.

Ben only continued to look at her, and she dropped the oven mitt she had just used to open the grill lid.

This was not good.

"Should I turn them over?" Nathan asked, still trying to get her attention.

But Gwen was lost. It occurred to her that maybe Ben Crowe wasn't as angry and intense as she thought. No one else in the town had a problem with him. Everybody else let him keep to himself without question or qualm.

Yet she nitpicked at everything he did. With him standing on the other side of her sliding glass doors, holding a plate of sliced tomatoes, staring at her as if he couldn't get himself to stop, Gwen suddenly knew why they didn't seem to get along and she squeezed her eyes shut.

He found her as attractive as she found him.

And he was fighting it every bit as hard as she was fighting it.

If it hadn't been for Nathan, dinner might have been eaten in complete silence. Luckily, neither Gwen nor Ben had trouble talking to Nathan. Luckily, Nathan didn't seem to notice that the adults were so uncomfortable with each other they were using him to pass the salt so they didn't have to speak directly to each other.

Being a gentleman, Ben helped with the dishes. The gesture reinforced that Ben Crowe was a very good man, but, unfortunately, it also reaffirmed the sexual attraction Gwen felt sizzling between them. She couldn't stop noticing that he wasn't merely a handsome man, he was a well-built man. She'd never seen him in a dress shirt and trousers, only a work shirt, vest and jeans. As he walked around her kitchen, putting away dishes and storing leftover food, his lighter weight apparel showed off his broad shoulders and his back which tapered into a trim waist. When Gwen realized that, she recognized her eyes were moving toward territory that was definitely off limits, and she refused to let herself even glance in his direction anymore.

When he shipped Nathan upstairs to get his jacket, Gwen also deduced that Ben had offered to help with the dishes so they would be too busy to be awkward around each other. Without the distraction of Nathan or the dishes, a thick silence stretched between them. Both tried to talk, neither could think of anything to say, and the peeks they stole at each other were so obvious and so telling, Gwen wanted to crawl into a hole and never come out.

She nearly breathed a sigh of relief when Nathan jogged down the steps. "I'm ready," he called, darting toward the door.

Obviously grateful, Ben followed him, and, relieved to have them going, Gwen followed Ben. But when the energetic nine-year-old slipped beneath Ben's arm and out the door, suddenly Ben and Gwen found themselves face-to-face and alone again.

"Thank you for staying," Gwen said, and made the mistake of looking up into his eyes. Lord, he had gorgeous eyes. Nearly black and as bright as stars, they looked down at her, pinning her into immobility.

"I appreciated dinner," he said quietly. "And also appreciated your being so good to Nathan."

"He's a wonderful boy," she agreed softly.

Ben's gaze fell to her mouth, then returned to her eyes, and Gwen watched him swallow hard. For a fleeting second she feared that he would kiss her, then realized she wished that he would. What would it feel like to have that beautiful mouth pressed to hers?

Ben cleared his throat. "I've sort of taken him under my wing, so if he gives you trouble, call me."

Gwen shook her head. "He's no trouble," she said. *But you are,* she thought, then realized that wasn't true. This man couldn't hurt her if she didn't let him. If she got control of these odd, runaway feelings right now, there would be no problem between them. She took a step back, away from him, clearly telling him she didn't want to be kissed.

He rubbed his hand across the back of his neck. "Thank you for dinner," he said, being formal again.

"Make sure your door is locked," he added before he walked outside. He closed her door with a secure tug, and then the only sound Gwen heard was silence.

She listened to the engine of his truck start, listened as the noise spiraled into nothing as he drove away, then squeezed her eyes shut and groaned. What the hell was happening to her? How could she have been so stupid as to stare in his eyes like a lovesick puppy?

For heaven's sake, how could she even be *looking* at another man when she wasn't over the last one yet?

Besides, she was pregnant. She was fat. She didn't even really walk anymore, she waddled. Just like with the cookies, the only person she was fooling was herself if she thought a gorgeous man like Ben Crowe would find her attractive in this condition!

Ben couldn't have disagreed more. Driving Nathan home that night he realized that the thing that struck him about her was how happy she was. She seemed to blossom around Nathan, which proved she would be a wonderful mother. But even before Nathan entered the picture Ben had noticed that Gwen...well, glowed. Yesterday it was so obvious he couldn't miss it. And tonight she virtually radiated light and energy.

He would have berated himself for staring at her all evening like some lovesick teenager, except when he saw her staring at him through the sliding glass doors, he realized she found him attractive, too. At first that had been nothing but good for his ego, then Ben reminded himself of his thoughts from the day before. Being attracted to an already pregnant woman wasn't something to play around with.

The next morning, bundled in denim and shielding his eyes from the sun with a Stetson as he rode the fence to spend some time outdoors—since he'd wasted the previous day in offices with lawyers, accountants and brokers—Ben decided that Gwen's pregnancy was the bottom line to everything. Since he hadn't been overwhelmingly attracted to a woman like this in years, and the biggest difference between Gwen and all the other women he met was her pregnancy, he figured that silly glow of hers was the real culprit, not an actual attraction.

He even felt fortified enough to knock on her door and walk right into her house that evening when he arrived to pick up Nathan. But when he saw her lying on the sofa, looking exhausted—completely without glow—and still thought she was the most beautiful woman in the world, he knew he was going to have to rethink this whole deal.

"What's up?" he asked, sitting on the edge of the sofa beside her tummy, so he could get a better look at her face.

"I'm fine," she said, obviously exasperated. "I told you before, I'm pregnant, not sick."

"Where's Nathan?"

"He's making dinner."

"He is?" Ben asked, his voice resonating with fear at the combination of a nine-year-old, boiling water and fire.

"Relax," she said. "It's only cold cereal from a box, but at this point that's all I have the energy to eat. He told me he can get something at home with his foster parents."

"I'll see that he gets dinner," Ben said, then rose from the couch. "And you're eating something more than cold cereal."

"Cold cereal is fine."

He snorted a laugh. "Not hardly. Have you ever read one of those labels? You're eating sugarcoated sugar."

The words were barely out of Ben's mouth before Gwen gasped as if in pain. He fell to the sofa again. "What's wrong?" he asked urgently.

She gritted her teeth from the discomfort, but said, "It's nothing."

"Oh, yeah, right," Ben said, rising from the couch. "Nathan, give me a hand here. I'm taking Mrs. Parker to the doctor."

With surprising strength, Gwen caught his hand and tugged him down to the sofa again. "You are not taking me to the doctor."

Leaning over so that he nearly pressed his nose to her nose, he disagreed. "Guess again."

"The baby is moving. That's all. Sometimes when he does it I get heartburn. Other times, like now, it just hurts like the dickens. It all depends on what he sits on."

She said the words quietly, softly, and very, very slowly and with every puff of breath that came from her mouth he realized how close they were. If he thought he'd been on the verge of kissing her the night before, he was in even worse shape tonight. First, she looked tired and alone. That right there deserved a kiss. Add her natural beauty to that and Ben found himself losing the battle.

"I still think I should take you to the doctor," he whispered, his voice shivery and hoarse because he realized he was bending closer and closer, so near her mouth now that his lips were almost touching hers.

He'd never felt so drawn to kiss anyone. Not because she was attractive, not because he was attracted to her, but because it felt right. She wasn't merely beautiful, she was sweet, and he wanted to taste some of that sweetness. He could feel himself being pulled toward her, confirmation, almost, that this was something he couldn't control.

But in the last second before their mouths would have touched, she said, "No."

Chapter Three

"No."

"No?" He didn't know if she'd said no to the kiss or no to going to the doctor. But he did know that he couldn't remember the last time anyone argued with him, and he nearly tripped himself when he bounced off the couch. "What do you mean, no?"

"Ben," she said patiently. "I gained twenty pounds in seven months...actually more like five months because I didn't gain anything the first two months. Picture my small frame suddenly getting twenty pounds, most of it in my middle."

He could. Clearly. He could see her standing in front of a mirror, wearing something soft and filmy, looking feminine and motherly and absolutely gorgeous. That's what bothered him. He could easily envision how she would do anything, from the simple to the sublime, as if he'd known her for years instead of weeks.

"I'm not sick. I'm tired. I do not need to see a doctor. I need a few minutes of rest, that's all."

When she put it like that, Ben believed her. But she wasn't completely out of the woods with him yet. "All right, you're not sick," he conceded gruffly, trying like hell to stifle the image she'd unwittingly forced him to create in his head. "But what you told me proves you need a good dinner."

She sighed. "I'm too tired to make a good dinner."

"No problem. Nathan and I will make one for you," he said, and turned toward her kitchen. "What would you like?"

"Steak and french fries," she said with a laugh. "But you don't have to make me dinner."

Walking to the door, he said, "You're not eating cold cereal. If you want steak, I'll make steak."

"I was teasing," she called after him. "If you insist on cooking, you don't have to go to that much trouble."

He stopped, faced her and skewered her with a look. "Let's get one thing straight. I never do anything I don't want to do, so if I volunteer to do something it's not trouble."

With that he left the living room, crossed the small entryway at the foot of the steps and went into her kitchen. "Nate, we need to make steak and french fries for supper. Do you have any idea where we can find those things?"

He nodded eagerly. "Sure, there's a freezer in the basement. She even has frozen fries."

"Great. You go get those and I'll start the grill."

With Nate's help dinner was ready in a little over half an hour. Just as Ben was preparing to put a tray together for Gwen, she entered the kitchen.

"This smells wonderful," she said.

Ben studied her critically. Her cheeks had color. Her energy appeared to have returned. She was smiling. "I knew a good meal would revive you. Just smelling it put color back in your face.''

"I was tired,'' Gwen said. "It's not a crime. I'll bet even you get tired, Ben Crowe.''

He shrugged. "I remember one time, when I was younger, I did get a little tired,'' he teased. "But the next day I came down with the flu, so we never really knew if I was tired or if that fluke day was actually just the beginning of my illness.''

"Oh, yeah, right,'' Gwen said, sitting at one of the place settings Nathan had arranged at the table.

"Seriously,'' Ben said as he served the steak, "you do look much better, and I'm sure you'll feel better once you eat.''

"Yeah,'' Nathan agreed, climbing onto the chair beside her. "You look better.''

Ben was abundantly relieved Nathan had taken the seat beside Gwen until he realized that sitting across from her would put them face-to-face. But as they ate, and as he watched her become more animated and more energetic, Ben was glad he could see her. He believed her when she said she was tired. He also believed that having a baby move inside you could cause pain. Still, it was good to have all that confirmed by the return of her high spirits and stamina.

As she and Nathan washed the dishes, Ben cleared the table, continuing to covertly watch her. Seeing her stretching to put the first glass on the appropriate shelf, he said, "Stack those below the cupboard and I'll store them.''

"Nonsense,'' she said with a laugh. "I can reach.''

"I know,'' Ben agreed, finally comprehending that the way to get this woman's cooperation wasn't through quibbling. If you argued with her, she tried to prove you wrong. So the best thing to do was to pretend to agree, then point her in the right direction. "It's faster if you make a stack to put away all at once, because you eliminate steps."

"What are you? Some kind of efficiency expert?"

"What's an efficiency expert?" Nathan asked.

"Someone who tells other people what to do," Gwen said curtly.

"Someone who finds a better way to do things," Ben contradicted, but he laughed. Because laughter was another way to reach this woman. After spending two days with her, he recognized she liked to laugh, and she liked seeing other people laugh. So if that's what it took to swing her thinking around in the way he wanted it to go, that's what he would do.

She turned to place a dish in the cupboard, but as she reached up he caught the plate. He didn't take it out of her hand, just guided it to the countertop, and when she released it, he directed her hand to get the next one.

She gave him a curious look, but he didn't stop long enough for her to realize he was monitoring her every move. He walked to the stove to wipe it clean, surreptitiously observing her from his peripheral vision. When she started to put another plate into the cupboard out of habit, he simply stepped beside her, seized the plate and guided it to the stack beside the dish drainer.

"Are you this annoying with everyone?" she asked, her eyes narrowing as she glared at him.

"Absolutely," he said, but again he didn't linger. Since the plate was on the pile and she was reaching for another dish, he walked away, busying himself with straightening her tablecloth. Once she and Nathan had finished washing and drying the few dishes and utensils used for their dinner, but before she got the chance to hoist them to the shelves above her, Ben shifted her attention to the table.

"Would you arrange those flowers?" he asked. "I think I messed them up when I returned the centerpiece to its place."

Though he thought she might have questioned that, she looked at the centerpiece, giving Ben enough time to quickly stash her stacks of dishes and glasses into the cupboard. By the time she turned and said, "How can you mess up a bunch of wildflowers?" he had everything put away.

"My mistake," he said. "Come on, Nathan, let's go."

Because she hadn't noticed that he had more or less manipulated her out of disagreeing about who would do what in the kitchen, Ben knew he had been successful. He also knew that dinner and company had boosted her spirits. He had not intended to get involved with her, but, really, somebody had to. Not because she was an invalid, but because she was alone. A million and ten things could happen to her and no one would be around to even discover her, let alone rescue her. So if Ben made himself and Nathan her protectors for the next few months, he wasn't doing anything but being a good neighbor. Besides, he was her landlord. He had a responsibility to make sure she was safe while she was on his property.

"I'll bring Nathan around at eight tomorrow morning," he announced as he grabbed his coat from a peg by the door and urged Nathan to do the same.

Gwen gasped. "No, you won't! It's one thing to have him come over after school, but a boy needs his Saturday to play. He doesn't need to be baby-sitting me. I told you. I'm perfectly fine."

Ben knew he could have found a way to contradict that without insulting her so Nathan would have the chance to earn his ten dollars, but he didn't have to because Nathan said, "But I like coming here. I'd rather be with you."

Instantly, he saw that the innocent tone of Nathan's voice, coupled with the sincerity of his words, hit Gwen right in the heart. She swallowed hard. "I like having you here."

"Then it's settled," Ben said. Not giving anyone a chance to think about it too much for fear of a change of opinion, he reached for the doorknob.

"But I'm not an invalid," Gwen said, the defensive comment pulling Ben's hand away from the door and causing him to face her again.

"I just like company."

"Right," he concurred guilelessly. He already knew that arguing with her only made her want to prove her points, so no matter what she said, he would agree.

"Right," Nathan said, too, apparently catching on to the same things Ben had.

"You're not sick. You just want company," Ben repeated to be sure she knew they understood her. Because, he supposed, in a way they did. She wasn't ill. But she also shouldn't be alone. They all agreed on that.

He just couldn't get too attached to her, which would be the tricky part if he had to spend too much time watching her smile, listening to her soft voice and enjoying the very fact—so clearly demonstrated by her pregnancy—that she was a woman.

The next morning, Gwen awoke bright-eyed and bushy-tailed. She felt wonderful, refreshed, alive, and she was waiting with French toast and tea when Ben dropped off Nathan.

The little boy entered the unlocked front door without knocking. "Hi."

"Hi," Gwen said. "Where's Ben?"

"He can't come in. He's got work to do."

When disappointment swamped her, Gwen wondered if her good mood hadn't been caused by knowing she would be seeing Ben that morning. But she told herself she couldn't let that be true. She wasn't in the market for another man. She couldn't be. The ink was hardly dry on her divorce papers. Getting involved with another man should be the last thing she wanted to do.

But as she served breakfast, she couldn't stop the small debate going on in her head about why Ben might have chosen not to come in with Nathan. While she and Nathan ate their French toast and drank their tea, she considered that he really might have work to do. But she countered that by speculating that she might have repulsed him by being so grouchy the night before. The debate went around and around until Gwen knew the only way she would stop the madness would be to take her mind off things with work. A few hours of occupying herself with earning a living were exactly what she needed. But since she felt duty-bound to entertain Nathan, she didn't see how she could do that.

After doing the dishes and enduring the internal argument about Ben for another fifteen minutes, Gwen knew she didn't have a choice. She had to work.

"Come on, Nathan," she said, directing him to the sunroom at the back of the cottage, the space she used for an office.

As they entered the cluttered area, Nathan glanced around in awe. "Wow!" he said, fingering her drafting table as if it were solid gold.

"You like to draw?" she asked.

"Do I ever!" he said, and turned those big brown eyes on her again.

"Good." She reached for some older chalk, colored pencils and a new tablet. "I can teach you anything you want to know. But first, this morning, we'll let you draw as many pictures as you want, the way you want to draw them, and we'll see what you need to learn. And we'll also see where your natural talents lie.''

He looked at the art supplies she was handing him and blinked up at her. "All this is mine?''

"Sure. But you have to keep them at my house. Because this is where you'll be doing your lessons.''

He nodded, reverently glanced at the supplies, then peered up at her as if stunned by her generosity. "Thanks.''

Gwen was struck again by the way this little boy appreciated everything she did for him. Because she had spoken with his foster mother to let her know that she had invited Nathan to visit her every day, she knew the woman genuinely cared for him, but she could also hear the age in his caretaker's voice. An energetic, intelligent boy like Nathan needed to be challenged. And though Gwen wouldn't take anything away from his foster parents, knowing that they cared for him and were doing the best they could, she vowed to continue providing as many opportunities for Nathan as possible without overstepping her boundaries.

As if he understood that Gwen couldn't be disturbed while she finished her projects, and also having accepted the task of providing samples of his abilities for her inspection, Nathan worked quietly. His presence was not the distraction Gwen feared it might be, but more than that, she soon found that having him in the room with her was a comfort of sorts. Like Nathan, she labored industriously and without a break until her back began to ache.

She recognized she'd worked too long at the same moment that she heard Ben's truck pull into her gravel lane.

Looking at the clock and seeing that it was past noon, she groaned.

"Oh, Nathan, I'm sorry."

He peeked up. "What?"

"I keep losing track of time, and one of these days I'm going to starve you to death. It's already past lunch, and we haven't had a break." Another thought struck and she groaned again. "And I don't have anything out of the freezer to make, either."

"That's okay," Nathan said, kneeling on the ledge built in front of the wall of glass to create something of a window seat. "Ben's bringing big bags of stuff."

"He's brought lunch?" she asked, peering over Nathan's head so she could see.

"Looks like," Nathan said.

They scrambled out of the sunroom to the front room to get the door for Ben because he had his hands full. As he stepped inside, Gwen saw the yellow bread wrapper hooked over the rim of the top of the brown paper bag.

"You didn't have to do this," she said immediately.

"What did I tell you yesterday?" Ben asked, depositing his packages on her table. "I don't do anything I don't want to do. So if I do something it's because I wanted to."

"Right," she said, though she still felt uncomfortable.

"Okay," Ben said. "I brought salami and Swiss cheese, bologna and roast beef. Which do you want?"

"Roast beef," Gwen said, unconsciously sitting down as Ben pulled his purchases from the brown bags. "I think that's probably the only one of those I can eat without getting heartburn."

"I'll make a note of that," Ben said, arranging the cold cuts and bread on the table in front of him. Then he removed a bag of cookies.

"Oh, chocolate twirls," Gwen said, her mouth watering. "I love those."

"Good," Ben said. "Nathan, how about checking the refrigerator for mustard."

"Bottom shelf," Gwen said, hardly realizing the men were waiting on her, though she did notice that it didn't seem as if there was anything for her to do.

"What do you like on your sandwich?" Ben asked.

She shrugged. "I can make my own sandwich."

"I already have the bread on a plate," he said, displaying the paper plate holding two slices of bread. "I know you want roast beef, but do you want anything else?"

"Put a piece of cheese on," Gwen said. However, the minute the words were out of her mouth, she recognized she was letting him make her sandwich. "I can do that."

"Done," Ben said, and handed her the paper plate.

"Thanks," Gwen said, but she started to rise. "I'll make coffee."

"I brought cola," Ben countered, producing it from a bag on the chair beside him. "You get glasses, Nate."

Nodding vigorously, the little boy jumped from his seat, opened the cupboard and was back at the table with glasses in seconds.

Gwen started to sit again, but seeing Ben open the mustard, she changed directions. "You'll need a knife for that."

He eased her back down. "Nate can get that. Right, Nate?"

"Right," Nate said, then ran to her silverware drawer. He extracted a knife and presented it to Ben.

"What kind of sandwich would you like?" Ben asked Nathan.

"Bologna," he said with a grin.

"Just bologna? Nothing else?"

"Just bologna."

All in all, making the sandwiches, distributing potato chips, pouring the cola and settling everyone into a seat took less than ten minutes. But Gwen wasn't oblivious to the fact that she'd done nothing to put this little impromptu lunch together.

Which, as hostess, made it all the more important that she come up with some good mealtime conversation. "So what did you do this morning?" she asked Ben, then mentally chastised herself because that hardly sounded interesting, let alone stimulating.

"I'm having trouble with my accountant," he said simply, then downed half a glass of cola. "But it's not a big deal. If he's messing up, I can fire him and replace him in a minute. I just don't like to get rid of somebody who doesn't deserve to be let go. I like to be sure."

"Good idea," Gwen agreed. "I've never been on the firing side of being an employer, but I'll bet it's no picnic."

"It doesn't have to be a disaster, either," Ben said. "The only real problem I ever had was firing someone unfairly. That will keep you up at nights and make you just plain miserable. I'll never do it again."

Though she didn't know Ben very well, certain things about his character were obvious. "I can't imagine you letting somebody go without good reason."

"Oh, I did," Ben assured her. "I found out too late I'd gotten bad information from someone who had a grudge against the guy."

"Yikes."

"Yeah, you've got to be really careful about who you trust," Ben agreed. "Anyway, I had to hunt the man down and bring him back with a raise. But in the end my conscience was clear.''

Ben's comment about trust didn't escape Gwen's notice. If she'd been romantically interested in him, she would have taken it as something of a warning. Since she wasn't romantically interested in him—couldn't be—she focused on the fact that Ben's generosity was only outdone by his integrity. Then she glanced at Nathan, saw he had finished his sandwich and was just about to ask him if he wanted another, when Ben beat her to it.

''All done, Nate? Or would you like something else?''

''More chips,'' he said, and Ben promptly complied with the request.

Gwen stifled a laugh. The way they interacted was cute, but more than that it was now obvious that they were deliberately keeping her from doing anything. Which was kind of sweet, though very impractical. She doubted they would stop if she told them she'd caught on, but she wasn't so stupid that she couldn't beat them at their own game.

''What are you doing this afternoon?'' she asked slyly.

''I'm going south to look at some horses.''

''Long trip?''

''It depends. If I find what I want at the first stop, I could be back before dinner.''

''Good. I'll be sure to make something that won't get cold or ruin if it sits while we wait for you.''

Ben's eyes narrowed as if he'd finally figured out she had tripped him up. She smiled ingeniously at him. His eyes narrowed another notch.

Deciding it best to change the subject as quickly as possible, Gwen said, ''Nathan and I started art lessons this morning.''

Ben shot Nathan a look, and though the little boy's eyes

widened, he said nothing. Ben continued to peer at Nathan, but his question was obviously addressed to Gwen. "You didn't do anything too strenuous, did you?"

"Even though I'm pregnant, I can still draw. Besides, I do it every day. Drawing textbook illustrations is how I make a living."

Seemingly content with the answer, Ben glanced at her. "Can't Nathan help you?"

"Not really. But even if he could, Nathan is busy with his own projects."

This time the look Ben shot Nathan was openly questioning.

"I'm making pictures," Nathan said apologetically.

"And I'm going to examine them so I can see what Nathan knows naturally and what he needs to be taught. I don't want to disturb his talent, but I do want to correct what he's doing wrong."

"Is this difficult?"

"Depends on what Nathan does and doesn't know."

"Do you have to stand?"

"Usually on my head when I judge a paper," Gwen said, tongue in cheek. "But it's really not hard."

Ben stared at her. "What in the hell are you talking about?"

Gwen laughed. "I'm teasing you, you idiot. Why don't you just paint a sign on my front door announcing that no one is supposed to bother me and that you don't want me to do any heavy labor."

"Good idea," Ben said, rising to begin putting leftovers away.

His answer only made her chuckle. He shook his head as if disgusted with her, but Gwen could see his lips twitching. He didn't mind being teased. In fact, it almost seemed he enjoyed it. She rose from her chair and began to gather the cold cuts.

"Nate can do that," Ben immediately protested.

"So can I," Gwen reminded him, then she sighed. "Really, I'm not going to like it if you don't let me do anything, and I catch on really quickly when I'm being tricked. So if I were you and I wanted to make sure I only did a minimum of work, I'd be a little more subtle and I'd also keep me busy with simple, easy tasks."

Ben burst out laughing. "I know we weren't that obvious."

"Sure you were," Gwen said, stashing the cola in her refrigerator. When she turned to the table, she saw Ben and Nathan working as a team to close the chips and bread and find a place to store them. The handsome dark-haired, dark-eyed man and the adorable little boy were so comfortable in her home that she felt peaceful and content for the first time in months. Without warning, her eyes misted.

"I'll put water in the basin to wash the dishes," she said quickly, and almost ran to the sink before either one of the men in her kitchen would see she was on the verge of tears. *Darn hormones,* she thought, grabbing the handle for the spigot.

"We have one knife and three glasses to wash," Ben said. "You don't need to do them now. We can do them with the supper dishes."

She realized that he intended to eat supper with her that night, and though she recognized it was only because he was keeping tabs on her, another wave of tears surged to her eyes. In her entire life she'd never had anyone worry about her. Forget about having someone who took care of her. She was competent Gwen. The girl who could handle herself. Even when her husband told her he didn't want her anymore, no one, with the exception of her cousin Hannah, even considered she might need comforting. Her wealthy parents' idea of handling the situation was to offer her a position on the Board of Directors of the family conglomerate. They never thought she might need a little TLC. And even if they had, they would have thought their offer of a board position to be proof that they loved her. They weren't the kind of people to hug or pamper her. If Gwen wanted something—even a letter of recommendation for college—she had to get it herself. But these two strangers had taken her in like a baby bird that had fallen from its nest. It was no wonder she was crying.

"There's no point in wasting water," Ben said, placing his hand over hers to turn off the spigot she was trying to turn on. Right hand on her upper arm, he started to shift her away from the sink, but she spun herself in the other direction, away from him.

"There, see?" he said, following her as she tried to make a graceful escape. "It's not so hard to listen to my instructions."

"Hmm-hmm," she said, blinking back tears. Emotions ran high in any pregnant woman, but a woman whose husband divorced her when she was carrying his child was doubly susceptible. She knew that. She planned for it. No matter what the catalyst for the tears, she could usually nip them in the bud by reminding herself that she could be proud of herself for how well she was doing here in Storkville. So why was it she couldn't stop today's uncontrollable urge to weep?

Was it because she was truly happy to have two people who seemed to care so much for her? Or because she was afraid she would lose them, too?

Or because she was becoming too dependent upon people she shouldn't depend upon? She'd learned long ago she couldn't count on anybody but herself, particularly not for emotional support. She'd broken her own rule with her ex-husband and gotten hurt. Now she was doing it again. Only this time with the most risky people of all. People upon whom she had no claim. Not even as friends, really, since she'd only known Nathan a few days and Ben a few weeks.

"Gwen, where are you going?" Ben called.

Though Gwen could have assured him that she wasn't about to do any difficult work, lift anything heavy or stand too long, she couldn't stop the waterworks forming behind her eyelids as easily as he'd turned off the spigot. It was embarrassing enough to be at the mercy of your hormones and emotions, without having to explain yourself to someone who might not understand. So she just kept moving. If he followed her, he probably wouldn't catch her until she was in the bathroom, and he would let her alone.

But Ben was a lot quicker than Gwen. He grabbed her hand and spun her around before she even reached the bottom of the steps. The action took her focus off controlling her tears, and just as quickly as he spun her around, Gwen burst into gut-wrenching sobs.

Chapter Four

Ben didn't waste a second. He pulled Gwen into his arms and cuddled her against his shoulder. But because that was about as far as his experience with a crying woman went, he glanced down at Nathan. "Now, what?"

Wide-eyed and baffled, Nathan shrugged. "I don't know."

"Oh, for Pete's sake," Gwen said, wiggling out of Ben's embrace. "It's hormones. This happens. Every once in a while all my emotions go haywire and I do something silly like cry. It's no big deal."

"You're sure?" Ben asked neutrally, though he felt a peculiar emptiness when she moved out of his arms.

"I can't control these tears because I'm tired from working this morning. In fact," she said, turning away from Ben, deliberately putting distance between them, intensifying the sense of loss he felt when she wiggled from his arms, "why don't you take Nathan with you when you leave so I can get a nap?"

Ben blinked in confusion over her swift change of

mood and attitude, but also because it appeared she was kicking him out. He almost admitted to being offended, but quickly convinced himself he wasn't hurt, simply surprised, and that was why he had an unusual tightening in his chest. But with that rationale he also concluded that if she meant nothing more to him than a neighbor in need, as he kept insisting, then he should be satisfied to respect her wishes and go, as she'd asked him to.

Baffled, cautious, Ben didn't have a clue what to say or do. Leaving like this felt awkward, inconsiderate, and just plain wrong. Particularly since he wasn't convinced she was as well as she said she was.

But while Ben ran the debate in his head, Nathan took the bull by the horns and did what needed to be done. "Are you sure you're okay?" he asked Gwen, sidling up to her until he was almost nestled against her.

Still a little teary-eyed, she gave the little boy a watery smile and ruffled his hair. "You have a lot to learn about women—especially pregnant women," she said, and Ben found himself agreeing heartily. He also found himself tight with nerves, waiting for her to confirm that she really was only tired, not upset, or worse, sick again.

"And I am tired," she added with another quick ruffle to Nathan's hair. "I need a nap."

Ben breathed a silent sigh of relief, but when he risked a glance at Gwen's face and saw the sadness in her eyes, another problem haunted him. Tired or not, it didn't seem right to leave her alone.

"Are you sure you don't want company while you sleep?" Nathan asked, and though Ben's mouth nearly fell open with amazement at the little boy's perceptiveness, he was once again glad Nathan had spoken for him.

Still, he held his breath—hoping for what, he wasn't sure—but Gwen only laughed and said, "Now, that would be a little silly, since I wouldn't know I had company while I was sleeping.''

Because Nathan was the one doing all the talking, he nodded sagely, but said, "Maybe somebody should come back and check on you."

This time Ben leaned forward, finally understanding that what he was hoping for was that she would want somebody to come back. Though she declined the offer, Ben decided right then and there he would be back to check on her whether she liked it or not.

He took Nathan home and ran a few errands, refusing to let his mind pursue the why behind this driving need to take care of Gwen. Pulling his truck into her driveway, he blocked every path of his mind as it tried to analyze this surge of protectiveness he was feeling for his new tenant. He didn't want to know why he felt compelled to do all these things. Whatever his reasons, the fact remained that Gwen was alone. So that made his reasons unimportant, insignificant and not worth chasing down.

Besides, he told himself as he knocked lightly on her front door, if he stopped thinking about why he wanted to do these things and simply did what had to be done, in the end when she didn't need him anymore, neither one of them would have any regrets.

Gwen didn't answer his knock, but Ben assumed she was sleeping. Confident that he was doing the right thing, as long as he didn't delve into the whys and wherefores of this situation, he took a block of wood and a knife from his truck and settled himself on her porch, where he began to create his own brand of art.

About an hour later when he heard her stirring, he took the wood back to his truck, returned to her porch and knocked again.

When she opened her door to him, Ben immediately

noticed that she looked much, much better. Maybe too good. With color in her face and sparkle in her eyes, she was back to being gorgeous again. Overtly feminine, yet healthy, strong and independent, Gwen was the epitome of the spirit of the American woman. Ben couldn't remember why he always felt she required protection.

"I just stopped to make sure you were okay," he said sheepishly, feeling foolish for this strange desire to hover over her when the truth was she didn't really *need* him.

"I'm fine," she said happily, and offered him entrance to her home. "Come in."

He shook his head. "No, that's okay. I just wanted to make sure..."

"That I was okay," Gwen said, finishing his sentence for him with a laugh. "How long have you been sitting out there, anyway?"

"About an hour."

"Well, the least I can do is make you a cup of coffee."

Ben decided there couldn't be any harm in that and accepted her invitation to come into her kitchen. But without the protection of Nathan he felt exposed and vulnerable. Still, remembering the way she looked when he left her, her eyes puffy from crying and her body sagging with fatigue, Ben stepped inside. If anyone was vulnerable, it was Gwen. Just because she seemed chipper and perky after a nap, that didn't mean everything was okay.

"Do you always get tired like that?"

"Sure," she said with a shrug as she filled the coffee filter with grains. "Not only does the baby use my energy, but remember I've also gained twenty pounds. You try strapping twenty pounds to your stomach and see if you don't tire easily."

Ben couldn't help it, he laughed. Stetson in hand, he took a seat by her table. Though the conversation between them trailed off, he didn't notice because he was trying to understand what it would feel like to suddenly carry twenty extra pounds. He didn't see how her small tummy could weigh that much and realized she must have been much thinner before she got pregnant. He also decided some of that weight must have been needed because she certainly wasn't fat. Her arms were thin and her legs were shapely....

Thinking about her body, he felt the stirrings of attraction again and reprimanded himself for noticing things about her that he shouldn't. But when she turned her back to him to reach into the cupboard, his gaze slid down the length of her legs exposed beneath the hem of a simple blue dress, and he knew he couldn't help himself. Being aware of her seemed as natural as breathing. There was something about her. Something different. Something *real*.

He tried to convince himself that she was "real"—very earthy and very feminine—only because she was pregnant, but part of him disagreed. She was a naturally warm, beautiful woman. Even her cottage reflected her soft, nurturing nature.

Without warning, he thought of his own big house, wood, leather and brass, nothing warm, nothing too personal, and he felt a burst of loneliness. He automatically tried to squelch it, but found that it wouldn't go down or go away as easily as it usually did.

"Oh, my goodness, look at the time. It's after five." She turned from the coffeepot and faced him with a smile. "I should be offering you dinner."

"That's not necessary," he said quickly, formally.

She shrugged. "I know." She paused long enough to pull her lower lip between her teeth, then caught his gaze and said, "But I like the company."

"Then I wouldn't mind eating somebody else's cooking besides my own," he said, returning her smile.

He knew acquiescing to her offer of dinner wasn't too smart, but he convinced himself that he didn't want to risk her getting upset again like she had that afternoon. But the truth was he liked her. He just liked being around her.

"Good, then you won't mind if I ask a favor."

He stiffened. "What favor is that?" he asked carefully.

She grinned. "I hate the steps to the basement of this cottage, but my freezer is down there. Could you get a package of pork chops out for me?"

Laughing, Ben rose. "At your service, ma'am," he said, then went into her basement and retrieved the frozen meat. On the return trip to the kitchen he decided she didn't like to go into her basement because there was no banister for the steps. He also decided that as her landlord he was duty-bound to fix that.

He handed her the pork chops and she thawed them in the microwave. Recognizing that preventing her from helping with lunch that afternoon might have caused her to feel inadequate and that could have led to her uncontrollable tears, Ben took his seat again to physically show her that he didn't think her incapable of caring for herself. In silence, he watched her assemble ingredients for their dinner.

"I guess you didn't go for your horses this afternoon?" she asked, her back to him as she worked.

"No," he said, downplaying the significance of that. "Tomorrow's another day."

She peeked at him. "Tomorrow's Sunday."

"If they want to sell me a horse, they'll open their doors to me on a Sunday."

She nodded. "I guess that's what you have to do when

you're in business for yourself," she said, and Ben realized she didn't have a clue about him or his place in their community. He also realized that might be part of what he liked about her. She saw him as a real person. Because she hadn't been a resident of Storkville very long, she didn't see him as the "local hero," the Native American boy who'd made something of himself. When she looked at him, she only saw a man.

All his life he worked for power and position. He got rich through wise investments and some very profitable real estate deals. Then he used his money and the help of high level friends he made along the way to not only get richer, but also to make sure his opinions counted with the politicians in the community. People respected him and treated him with honor because he was intelligent and influential which was exactly what he had sought to achieve. And the first woman to really catch his interest was the one person who didn't know a thing about his power and position. She liked him for himself.

He hadn't realized how important that was, how good that would feel.

Gwen hadn't realized how good it would feel to have someone who not only appreciated her pregnancy and cared about her well-being, but who was smart enough to step back and let her handle things for herself every once in a while.

Watching Ben out of the corner of her eye, Gwen could see he was dying to jump in and help her, but he respected her enough to let her make dinner alone. Everything he felt was clearly evident in his eyes and sometimes even apparent in the way he stiffened or relaxed. At first all the emotion that poured from him puzzled her. Now that she was getting better at reading and understanding the man at her table, Gwen concluded that knowing what a man was thinking and feeling might have saved her from marrying the wrong man.

The mere fact that she could draw that conclusion showed her that her life with her ex-husband had been a farce. Nothing like what she'd thought it was going to be. Nothing like what she wanted. She'd recognized all along that divorcing Tim, though painful, had been the right thing to do, but this evening she was really beginning to understand why.

Looking back on the events of her marriage with the perspective provided by some time away, she was even starting to wonder if Tim hadn't married her for her family's wealth and prestige, and conveniently grabbed on to the pregnancy as an excuse to divorce her when he discovered she not only didn't take money from her parents she seriously didn't want to lead a life like theirs.

Though Gwen's kitchen was quiet through most of her dinner preparations, it wasn't an uncomfortable silence. Ben appeared to be thinking about something important, and since she wanted a little thinking time to make peace with her new feelings about her divorce, Gwen didn't mind the lack of noise. She broiled her pork chops, prepared a side dish with noodles and buttery garlic sauce, added some frozen vegetables and even checked to be sure she had cookies for dessert.

Somewhere in the middle of her preparations, Ben rose and began to set the table. Again, they worked in a silence that wasn't strained, but more like companionable. If Gwen had thought *that* the whole way through, it probably would have scared her to death. Which was why she didn't think it through. Every time her mind tried to travel down that alley, she shifted her thoughts in another direction.

"So what did your husband do for a living?" Ben asked when they sat down to eat.

She shrugged. "He was an accountant who worked for a corporation."

"That's...nice," Ben said.

"It was boring," Gwen contradicted. "Not his job per se, but the life-style."

Ben pinned her with his no-nonsense stare. "If life with him was boring, why did you marry him?"

"I loved him. And at first life wasn't boring. I kept thinking we were doing what we had to do until we could afford to do what we wanted to do. I didn't mind dinner with business associates." She smiled. "I didn't even mind kissing up as long as I didn't have to do it too often."

"But," Ben prodded when she fell silent.

"But then Tim suddenly got very critical and very demanding." She shrugged. "I found myself compromising over everything. If I hadn't accidentally gotten pregnant I might have compromised myself out of a family."

Ben stared at her. "Now you've lost me," he said, baffled and confounded like never before. But having already made the connection that he liked the way she treated him as a normal person, Ben took that hypothesis one step further. He deduced that she treated him the same way his friends had treated him before he suddenly became one of the wealthiest, most powerful people in the county. Since that was the case, he decided to return the favor and to treat her as a friend, too.

And if they were going to be friends, he needed to understand this failed relationship of hers.

"How could he get you to give up having a family?"

"My husband didn't want kids."

"You told me that," Ben conceded with a nod.

"And my husband always got what he wanted. Especially from me."

Thinking about how Gwen fought him every step of the way, Ben chuckled. "I find that hard to believe."

"Because I'm a little feisty?"

"That might have something to do with it."

"You can't fight something you don't see coming," Gwen said. "Tim never did anything in an obvious way, all his demands were subtle. Basically, he used criticism as a means of manipulation. And one day I woke up and found myself living in a town house in Georgetown, rather than a small house in the country in Virginia."

"There's nothing wrong with that," Ben suggested carefully.

She shrugged. "You're missing the big picture. I woke up one day and I was living in the city, working for a company when I wanted to be on my own freelancing as I am now, and even dressing differently. We ate out every night, belonged to a country club. We were supposed to be two people looking to make a difference in the world and ended up just like everybody else."

She shook her head, either still unable to accept it all, or not quite sure she was getting her point across. "It seems absurd now, but at the time, one compromise at a time, I didn't even see our lives were going in the wrong direction. But the day Tim told me he didn't want our baby and didn't want to be married to me anymore, I realized I wasn't surprised. I finally understood he had always been comfortable and happy leading the life we led, and I recognized that could only be because he had lied to me about what he wanted. When I figured that out it all started to make sense to me."

It all made sense to Ben, too. Hadn't he been there himself? If his former girlfriend Julie hadn't left him, wouldn't he be in a city, confined to an office, belonging to a country club?

The thought alone almost made him laugh, but they were talking about Gwen now, not him. And he really wanted to understand.

"He even lied to you about wanting kids?"

"In the most hideous, unfair way." She caught Ben's gaze. "At one time we had our children's names chosen."

"What?"

"He was that good," Gwen explained. "He told me what I wanted to hear, all the while he charted an entirely different future. He even manipulated our circumstances to make it look like we had no choice but to stay where we were. So I never questioned the fact that we seemed to be going in the opposite direction from our original plans." She shook her head. "But he couldn't manipulate away a pregnancy. He knew better than to even try. And since I no longer fit the mold of his perfect life, he just kicked me out of the town house in Georgetown."

And hadn't Ben been there, too?

"He was an idiot," Ben said, then turned his attention to his pork chops. Because they were getting too close to his own humiliating rejection, and because he didn't want to get so caught up in agreeing that he might actually say something aloud, he changed the subject. "These are very good."

"Thank you," Gwen said, the not-so-subtle shift of subject not lost on her, but she was happy to see the topic go. Though she was glad to have the truth of her past out in the open, she didn't care to dwell on it. Not because it was painful to talk about. With Ben it was surprisingly easy. And that was the sticking point. They were getting too close. In three days, she felt more bonded to him than she had to Tim, and that was bad. She was pregnant with

Tim's child. She had a failed marriage she had only to-night come to terms with. She didn't want to inadvertently drag Ben into all her problems.

"So, what do you do for entertainment around here at night?" Ben asked her, when they had finished their meal and were preparing to wash the dishes.

"Read mostly," Gwen said, pouring dish liquid into the basin in the sink.

Ben only asked the question to listen for the sounds of tiredness he expected to seep into her voice. Not hearing any, he wasn't sure whether he should be relieved, or worried since this might mean she wouldn't sleep that night. Now that he'd categorized her as not just a friend, but a friend of the type he had before Julie, before the money, before the power and prestige kicked in, he wasn't worried about his runaway feelings for her. Being concerned for a friend was perfectly natural.

"I could stay and play cards or a board game, if you'd like."

"No. That would be too much of an imposition. I'm fine."

"But you will let me help with the dishes?"

"Sure. Whenever anybody volunteers to help clean up, I don't turn them away."

Convinced that her answer proved she saw him as a friend, too, and that she wasn't making more out of this situation than it was supposed to be, Ben helped her to return her kitchen to its clean state.

"Now, before I go," he said, "is there anything you want out of the freezer for tomorrow?"

She thought for a second. "Probably something for both lunch and supper since I'm hoping Nathan comes over."

"I'll bring him over," Ben said casually.

"Don't make him come over if he doesn't want to."

"He adores you. And was worried sick this afternoon. Coming over tomorrow will be the best thing for him."

"Probably," Gwen agreed. "And it will give me a chance to spend some time with him and his drawings."

Again the conversation was normal and natural, taking Ben's comfort level another notch. He didn't know why he had been so worried about his feelings for this woman, except that he had needed to clearly label them. Now that he had termed them *friendship,* everything she did seemed to demonstrate that he was correct. They were friends. Someday, they would be good friends. Very good friends. He could feel it. He could see it.

Which also explained why he so clearly saw the future with her. She was part of his future—as a friend.

More comfortable than ever with his explanation, Ben went to her basement and retrieved the items she'd requested. As he reentered her kitchen, he said, "I'm going to put a rail on those steps. Then you probably won't be uneasy going down for yourself." A thought struck him and he added, "By the way, how are you doing your laundry if you don't like to use those steps?"

She smiled sheepishly. "Most days I go outside, walk around to the steps at the back of the house...."

"Which have a railing," Ben said, confirming his suspicions. She didn't like the indoor steps because there was nothing to hold on to as she walked down. "I'll fix this."

"I'd appreciate it," Gwen said.

This time it was Ben who felt the merry bubble of excitement in his stomach. It had been such a long, long time since he'd had a normal relationship with anyone, because it had been such a long, long time since anyone treated him as an equal. It felt so good, he didn't heed the danger signals when she walked him to the door. He didn't notice the undercurrent of warning in the joy that swamped him at being appreciated on such an elemental level. He didn't realize how good it would feel to be needed in such a personal, intimate way. He didn't realize how much he would like it. He didn't realize it would make him dizzy and reckless.

"What time should I bring Nathan tomorrow?"

"Nine is fine," Gwen said, smiling up at him. "But only if he wants to."

"He wants to," Ben insisted with a groan. "I had to promise I would call him the minute I get home tonight to let him know you're okay."

She shook her head in amazement. "You two. I keep telling you I'm only pregnant. I keep telling you most of my emotions are hormones. When are you going to get that through your thick skulls?"

He hooked his index finger under her chin and lifted her face until he could catch her gaze. "And when are you going to understand that we only worry about you because we like you?"

"I like you, too," she whispered.

"Good," Ben said. The temptation to kiss her swirled around him again. This time, however, he recognized it for what it was. The desire of one friend to comfort another. Or maybe the desire of one friend to show appreciation to the other.

His rationale firmly in place, Ben kissed her.

Chapter Five

He intended to brush his lips across hers lightly, a celebration of sorts of their blossoming friendship. But when his mouth touched Gwen's the recurrent magnetic pull he felt around her kicked in and he suddenly needed to get closer.

But the moves he made didn't satisfy, only seemed to entice him to the next step, and in the end the light brush became a tentative press. The press became a nibble, the nibble turned into a hungry, openmouthed kiss, and the hungry, openmouthed kiss became a full-scale assault.

Though she kissed him back as fervently and as eagerly as he kissed her, Ben knew he nonetheless controlled this situation. He told himself he could stop at any minute. And when that didn't pull him away, he *advised* himself to stop immediately. But he couldn't seem to listen. Up to this point he'd always felt drawn to her, magnetically pulled to her, but right now what he felt was driven. And hungry. And maybe even a little bit greedy.

She tasted as sweet as he knew she would, and kissing

her was pure joy. Not just pleasure, but joy. He supposed it might have been because this kiss had started out as a celebration of a new friendship, more an emotional expression than a physical one, but whatever the reason the kiss was good. He felt, he savored, he tasted every nuance. The feeling of her wrapped in his arms, the flavor of her mouth, the wonder at the surge of arousal pumping through him from a mere kiss. He felt it all.

And when he pulled away, one quick peek in her eyes told him it had been the same for her.

"Wow."

She paced a step away from him. "You can say that again."

It took every ounce of control Ben had not to blow his breath out in disbelief or to rub his hand across the back of his neck the way he did when he was confused or frustrated.

What the hell was that?

"I didn't mean for that to happen. I didn't want it to go that far...."

Gwen gasped. "You think I did?"

"No, no!" he said, giving in to the urge to run his hand across the back of his neck. "I kissed you because I like you as a friend. Somehow things got carried away—probably my fault," he added because he knew it was. "But it won't happen again."

From the stricken expression on her face when she took another step back, Ben promised himself it definitely wouldn't happen again.

He grabbed his hat from the peg by the door. "I'll bring Nathan over tomorrow morning," he said, then left because he knew any more conversation would only make things worse than he had already made them.

And they were a mess. Since he was committed to

bringing Nathan over to help her, he had to see her and deal with her every day. Now that would be awkward. All because of a bunch of hormones and emotions he couldn't understand, much less control.

But from here on out, he wasn't going to underestimate them. If he couldn't control them, he would stay the hell away from her. He would find a way to get Nathan to her house and take him home again with a minimum of contact between himself and Gwen. She didn't need a combination of confirmed bachelor and jaded loner in her life. What she needed was stability and security.

That night Gwen dreamed about Ben. They lived together in a house so ornate and grand it could only be described as a palace. Relaxed and happy, they seemed to float on air and their castle was filled with contentment. Everything about their life together was wonderful.

When her alarm sounded, she bounced up in bed, weak with need and her heart pounding, and she chastised herself the whole way to the bathroom. She knew the symbolism. She didn't have to be Freud to recognize she was beginning to see Ben as her Prince Charming, and that wasn't good. True, the kiss from the night before showed there was more between them than friendship—or *could be* more between them than friendship, she corrected, refusing to jump the gun in this relationship—but right now she had to stick with the simple facts.

They were friends, who might turn into more than friends. But that was as far as it went. Particularly since Ben seemed as astounded as she had been by the intensity of their kiss, and in the heat of the moment had said he wouldn't kiss her again. All that being considered, Gwen had to concede there might be no relationship blossoming between them.

Still, she dressed carefully in her newest maternity jeans and a thick angora sweater she'd bought to spoil herself one day when she was feeling blue. She convinced herself she'd only done these things because it was Sunday, not because she was trying to dress up for Ben. But when Ben's truck drove into her driveway, Nathan jumped out and the truck roared away again, she had to stop herself from getting upset, and then she knew she *had* dressed up for Ben.

"Hi, Gwen."

"Hello, Nathan," she greeted cheerfully as he entered her front door. "Ben not coming in?" she asked, careful to keep her tone neutral both for Nathan and herself. Ben might have a good reason for not coming in, and if he did she had no cause to be upset. She had to deal with the truth, because guessing about his intentions or assuming things that were wrong would either embarrass her or ruin everything.

Nathan shrugged out of his jacket. "He said he's got stuff to do."

"Just stuff?"

"Just stuff."

The wave of disappointment that washed over her was heavy enough that Gwen almost sat down, but didn't. First, she didn't want Nathan to see she was disappointed. Second, she had to get a hold of herself. The very fact that Ben couldn't even stop in to say hello after kissing her passionately the night before physically explained what he had tried to say when he left. He believed the kiss was a mistake. And he hadn't changed his mind after a night of thinking about it. This relationship wasn't going any further. He wasn't her Prince Charming.

"Ben always has stuff to do," Nathan said, pulling out

a chair as he pulled Gwen back into the present with his comment.

"A ranch must be a busy place," Gwen agreed. "How's oatmeal and toast for breakfast?"

"Good. But Ben doesn't do a lot of things on his ranch."

Reaching for the bread, Gwen stopped and faced Nathan. "Then what does he do?"

"Everything," Nathan said with a laugh. "Everybody asks him to do stuff."

Because she was stretched halfway up the length of the cupboard, on a course to retrieve the oatmeal, Gwen again stopped midway and faced Nathan. "He spends his life doing favors?"

"Sort of."

Curious, but in a way that gave her tingles of recognition she wasn't sure she liked, Gwen licked her dry lips, then said, "Does he walk dogs? Does he fix porches? Does he pay rent? What kind of things?"

Nathan considered that. "He goes to the school a lot to talk, and he gives money to people. Especially to go to college."

"Oh," Gwen said, and this time she did take a seat by the table.

"You okay?" Nathan said, peering at her.

Gwen smiled. "Yeah, I'm fine," she said, and rose to make the oatmeal and toast, but she really wasn't fine. She felt stupid and thickheaded. These past few days she'd thought Ben Crowe spent time with her because he liked her—he had even said it—but the truth was she was only another person he helped. Though Nathan hadn't clearly explained Ben's life to her, Gwen understood. He was a highly successful man who spent his time encouraging others and taking care of the downtrodden.

She, unfortunately, was one of the downtrodden.

But not for long. She'd not only recovered from the loss of her marriage, the man she thought she loved and the future she thought she was getting, in these past months Gwen had strengthened herself enough to build a new life. And it was a good life. A happy life. There was no way on God's green earth she would throw away all that progress because she'd misinterpreted the intentions of a man.

Pasting on her best smile, she placed toast on the table in front of Nathan. "Do you want to go over your drawings today?"

He nodded enthusiastically. "You bet."

She put Ben Crowe as far out of her mind as she could put anybody or anything, until his truck came barreling into her driveway around eleven-thirty. When he jumped out, then reached in again to retrieve two brown grocery bags, Gwen squeezed her eyes shut. He was so obvious about only coming around to help her that Gwen couldn't believe she had thought his kindness might have deeper meaning—except to rationalize that the way he sometimes looked at her and the fact that he'd kissed her had weakened her ability to reason.

Watching him walk to her door, she forgave herself for being flustered and unfocused because he was such a handsome, sexy man. Tall and well built, dark and brooding, Ben Crowe was a veritable feast for female eyes. Men like him threw women for a loop all the time. She was as susceptible as everybody else was. She simply couldn't let her silly daydreaming go on any longer. She had to keep her wits about her and control herself.

And she also couldn't sit by idly and let him take care of her anymore.

"Hi," she said cheerfully, opening the front door for him. "What's this?"

"Lunch," he said simply, then strode to the table.

"Oh," she said, walking over to join him. Having the rugged masculine rancher in her kitchen immediately did strange things to her nervous system, confirming that his good looks—or more to the point, how she reacted to his good looks—was the problem. Last night, he might have recognized from her behavior or body language that she was attracted to him and concluded she wanted him to kiss her, so he kissed her—which corroborated the theory that he was actually taking his cue from her. If she couldn't find an easy way to get him to stop treating her as a charity case, she might have to explain that though she looked like a woman who wanted to be kissed, she didn't necessarily *need* to be kissed. Just like she might get hungry and frequently be lonely, but she didn't *need* him bringing her lunch, or *need* him spending all his free time with her.

But first she would try an indirect—hopefully safer and less embarrassing—approach of reminding him she could take care of herself.

"I was going to take Nathan to the diner for lunch today."

"Good, because that's what I brought," Ben said, as usual not missing a beat in subtly contradicting her when she tried to refuse his generosity. "I stopped at the diner and got three take-out meals. I hope you like meat loaf."

"I love meat loaf," Gwen said as the spicy aroma curled around her, teasing her senses and awakening her taste buds.

From Ben's quick rebound and from the way he was pulling things from bags, it was obvious he wasn't going to be easily dissuaded, and Gwen conceded she would have to try another tack to get him to stop babying her—but after she ate his meat loaf. Not only did it smell delicious, but also it had set her stomach to rumbling.

Besides, watching him work, seeing that he was inherently good and his intentions were honorable, Gwen got a pang of guilt. He was a darned nice guy and she didn't want to insult him. She just wanted to make sure they didn't make another mistake like the one they made the night before.

"Nathan and I will set the table."

"Why don't you have a seat while Nathan and I set the table?" Ben countered.

She shook her head. "Because I have all kinds of energy that I need to use," she said, realizing she'd found at least one path to get her point across to Ben without being insulting and without having to discuss that kiss. She couldn't even think about kissing this man without wanting to shiver. Now that he was in her kitchen, rugged and manly and serving her food, there was no way she could broach the subject of his kissing her without getting starry-eyed and maybe even swooning.

"Actually, Ben, you've seen my worst day. Friday night, when I couldn't seem to get off the sofa, that was the worst I've ever been. And the only real cause was fatigue." She said all that as she stretched into the cupboard to get dishes and brought them to the table.

"I take vitamins, have regular checkups, exercise enough to stay healthy without hurting myself, and I get a good eight hours of sleep every night." She didn't mention that her dream of the night before was peppered with references to him and symbolically depicted him as her Prince Charming, though she did feel a swell of disappointment recognizing that dream wouldn't come true.

But she squelched it. There was no way she'd pine over a man again.

"So you see, I'm perfectly capable of setting a table." *And doing everything else you seem determined to do for me,* she added silently, conveying the thought with the look she gave him when she caught his gaze.

He grunted noncommittally and turned away. "Nathan, go wash your hands."

"Yes, sir," the big-eyed little boy said obediently, and scampered away.

Ben began folding the brown paper bags in which their diner meals had been carried. Gwen continued to arrange the table. A long silence stretched between them. She considered that he might be uncomfortable about having kissed her, but discounted that idea immediately. In his mind, kissing her was just another favor of sorts. Add that to the few things he'd said before he bolted the night before—and, yes, she finally understood that he'd bolted the night before—and Gwen knew Ben had kissed her as a favor. From his hasty retreat she understood he recognized kissing her was above and beyond the call of duty, yet he was still here today, laying out her lunch, monitoring her safety.

Which meant he wasn't talking because he wasn't accepting what she kept telling him about being capable of doing things for herself. Rather than argue, he simply stayed silent—because she couldn't win an argument they didn't have. But like it or not, Gwen knew this was a discussion that couldn't be put off anymore.

"Ben, you no longer have to be my Boy Scout."

"Excuse me?"

"I think you heard me," Gwen said, her voice pleasant but firm. "All this is very nice," she said, sweeping her hand in the direction of the food on the table. "But you don't need to do it. There are plenty of other people in Storkville who need your help more than I do. Your time and your money are probably better spent elsewhere.''

''What in the hell are you talking about?''

''I'm talking about using your time, money and talent for a better cause. I don't need you.''

He shot her a confused look. ''Didn't I tell you that I do all these things because I want to?''

''Of course you do,'' she agreed. ''You take pleasure from caring for people, and you like me because I'm someone you can care for. But, really, Ben, it's not necessary.''

Obviously confused, Ben took a seat. He rubbed his fingers across his forehead as if thinking, then said, ''Let me get this straight. Somehow or another you think I come here to have lunch with you and Nathan because I'm trying to help you.''

''Exactly.''

''You don't think I come here because I enjoy your company—even though I kissed you last night?'' he asked, then caught her gaze.

She felt the heat of embarrassment rising to her cheeks, but nonetheless held her ground. ''No. You said yourself you didn't want to kiss me....''

''I said I didn't want the kiss to go as far as it did. I kissed you because I do like you.'' He paused, his dark eyes holding hers captive for a few seconds, then he added, ''But as a friend. Nothing more. That's what I was trying to tell you right after I kissed you. I don't want to get romantically involved, but I enjoy our friendship. That's why I'm here now. I wanted to stay away, but I couldn't. I like your company.''

''But Nathan said...''

"Ah, Nathan," Ben said as if he finally understood. "What has Nathan told you?"

"That you help a lot of people," Gwen said. "And that's good. But I don't need to be one of them. If you're only here because I'm someone you can take care of, find someone who needs you more."

She hadn't meant for the words to come out that harsh or that sharp, but they had. She watched Ben rub his hand across the back of his neck and knew he was carefully considering his answer.

"All right. First of all, I'm going to throttle Nathan. It's true I have a reputation for being a good guy, and I like that reputation. But you're the first person I've ever felt that I wasn't helping, per se, but more like sharing with. My house is big and lonely. You're company for me. But there are also days when I don't want to be everybody's hero. I appreciate coming somewhere, being with someone who treats me like a normal guy, not some sort of icon."

Embarrassed, Gwen sat on one of the chairs by the round table. That was certainly an angle she hadn't thought of. And certainly a darned good, nonsexual, platonic reason to enjoy her company. She was such a schoolgirl! Why did she always try to turn her relationship with Ben into something it wasn't?

"I'm sorry. You're more than welcome to come over any time you want. I like the company, too."

"Thank you," he said, sounding as uncomfortable at having to explain himself as Gwen felt at needing an explanation.

Again the silence stretched between them, but Ben suddenly chuckled.

"What?" Gwen asked, anxious for anything that would make her laugh and lessen her misery.

"There isn't a soul in town who would take me to task for buying her lunch," he said, then laughed heartily. "Hell, there isn't a soul in town who would take me to task, period." He reached over and cupped her cheek in his palm, lifting her face so she was forced to look at him. "And the funny part of this is, *that's* why I like you."

She had to admit that his explanation made her smile and even reduced her feelings of uneasiness. Because she had enough of her own problems, and didn't want the complications of a romance right now, either, she appreciated his assessment of their relationship. She liked him as a friend, but didn't want to get romantically involved. That was good. It worked for her, too, and it seemed to resolve the awkwardness for both of them.

But when he left, taking Nathan with him for a ride around the ranch to check on things, Gwen tried to focus on her current freelance project but couldn't. Instead, she rose from her seat by her drafting table and paced to the wall of windows.

Now that she didn't have to worry about the difficulties a romantic entanglement would cause for her, she remembered things from her conversation with Ben, especially the tone of his voice, and she recognized there was a lot she didn't know about this man who had decided to be her friend.

She wasn't entirely clear on how Ben had become Storkville's local hero. She remembered him telling her that his parents had abandoned him, but he'd never elaborated on that. She didn't even know who had raised him. So far, the only contact or connection she had seen that he had with the reservation was Nathan. Based on his appearance, she'd made the assumption that he was Sioux. But maybe there was more to the story?

And maybe he wasn't coming to her to give her help,

as much as he was subconsciously trying to get some help? Albeit it only understanding.

Hadn't he said she was the first person not to take his benevolence for granted? And hadn't he said he liked that about her?

She wasn't surprised that night when he returned to her house to check on her, but this time she was more ready. The bottom line, she decided, to Ben's being drawn to her was that she was a stranger. It was always easier to confide in someone you didn't know. Someone who wouldn't prejudge. Maybe he was looking for someone to listen to him for a change.

"Feel like having a sandwich?" she asked as she granted him entry. "Your cold cuts are still here."

He frowned at her. "You didn't eat those?"

"I only eat three meals a day like everybody else," she said, leading him toward the kitchen table, the focal point of the small cottage. "When I snack, it's a cookie."

"I'm sure that's good for the baby," he observed wryly.

Laughing, she shook her head. "You know nothing about nutrition. I make sure the baby and I get everything we need. It's the overflow calories I provide in cookies."

"Whatever," he said, batting a hand in dismissal and taking a seat by the table as she reached into the refrigerator to pull out the salami and cheese.

She noticed that he didn't even seem to realize he was letting her wait on him, and didn't say anything as she brought bread and mustard, cold drinks and cups to the table. For the first time in their relationship, she felt they had actually balanced out. Both of them were behaving the way they should be behaving.

Confirmation, she was sure, that this was the perfect

opportunity to drop a few questions about his past and let him know he could trust her with his answers.

"I hope you don't mind my asking," she said as she sat beside him at the round table, "but you're Sioux, right?"

Taking a bite of his sandwich, he nodded. "Hmm-hmm."

"Grow up on the reservation?"

He shook his head. "No…well, yes and no. When I was about eight, my mother moved to Ohio to find work, didn't do well and eventually put me into foster care. So, I had eight years at the reservation in my 'growing up' years. But the rest of the time, I was away."

Because the information was unexpected, it swam around in Gwen's head for a minute before she could fully digest it. But, once the facts settled, she realized they explained a good bit about the man Ben was today.

"Why'd you come back?"

He took a minute to chew and swallow his food, and Gwen suspected that might have been to give himself time to think about what he would say, maybe how he would say it, or maybe even how far go to with her. "My mother died."

"Oh, I'm sorry."

"It's been years, and frankly I didn't feel that I knew her when she died. The loss had been endured long before her actual death. I came home for the funeral as something like a formality." He paused, considered his next statement, then added, "I'd always thought my mother didn't want me. Because I was illegitimate, and my father was a married man, I thought I was something like the reminder of a mistake to her. A *constant* reminder of a mistake, and that was why she gave me up. That was what I grew up believing."

"When I came home for her funeral, I learned from her friends that she'd given me up to provide a better life for me. She struggled for years, most of the time hardly putting food on the table, and one day decided I deserved more. Giving me up was her way of giving me more."

"That was a very brave thing to do," Gwen whispered solemnly.

He shrugged. "Depends on your perspective. I felt abandoned. The first two days in foster care were the best of my life. Good food, solid, dependable people for caretakers, and visits from my mother." He paused, contemplating his next words, then said, "When the visits stopped and I discovered she'd gone back to the reservation, I felt abandoned."

"But you said your foster parents were good people...."

He looked her in the eye. "The person who was supposed to want me, didn't want me. The person who was supposed to love me, didn't love me. At eight that was how I saw it."

And didn't Gwen know all about that? Though she now recognized that getting out of the relationship with Tim was the best thing that could have happened to her, it still hurt to realize the person who was supposed to love her the most in the world didn't even want her around.

After a minute of thought, she nodded her understanding of both what he was saying and what he hadn't said. From the tone of his voice it was clear that though he still had scars about feeling abandoned, he wasn't bitter. He'd had enough time to examine the facts and to come to terms with them. For now, that was enough.

"So that's why I don't know as much about my heritage as I would like," Ben said, breaking the short silence with a change of subject. "I used to read a lot and spend time at the reservation, but I felt I was too far behind to ever catch up and I quit.''

"Was spending so much time at the reservation how you got your reputation for being a hero?''

Ben grinned. "Not hardly. Only the kids looked up to me. Most of the elders thought I was an idiot.''

"Why would they think you were an idiot?'' Gwen gasped.

"Let's just say I'm a slow learner. I couldn't catch on to what the rest of them knew simply by living.''

"It's always easier to learn a life-style by living it than by reading about it,'' Gwen agreed.

"No kidding,'' Ben said. They were quiet again for a minute or two, then Ben added, "I have a better reputation in town than I have at the reservation. But not because I sought to get one. I liked having influence, but kept most of my political interests and business deals private, then one day I innocently gave a donation to a community project. I have money and take my responsibilities seriously, so when another project came up, I gave again.''

He grinned with self-deprecation. "It was odd. Suddenly, everybody loved me. I'm not the kind of person to walk little old ladies across the street or to put in hours and hours of community service, so when everybody started throwing respect my way because of a little money, I clearly saw the value of a dollar. If even a loner like me could become a local hero, I knew money really did talk. Since my money was going to earn my reputation for me, I decided to make it say what I really wanted it to say and I established scholarship funds.''

Dropping his voice to a stage whisper, he beckoned her closer, then said, "I think that's what put me over the top. Especially with the kids.''

His silliness made Gwen laugh, but she also recognized

any other questions she might think of would have to wait. She felt a new empathy with Ben, a deeper friendship, a new comfort level because he understood the burden and responsibility of money, yet he still found a way to live a simple, happy life. Because of that empathy she knew that he wasn't the kind of man to tell all his secrets in one night. She considered herself lucky that he had confided this far, and contented herself with the knowledge that there would be other nights. Other talks. Private, intimate talks around her kitchen table.

The thought started a shiver of awareness to form, but she stopped it. She wondered if she would always have to remind herself that this was not a romantic relationship they were entering into, but a platonic one, then quickly told herself not to worry. There was a reasonable explanation for why she wasn't thinking clearly. Ben was so attractive and so much fun, he had nearly gotten her to forget about Tim, and that was where she was making her mistake. From here on out, every time she started feeling romantic things for Ben, she would think of her own relationship failure and that should be enough to scare her off men forever. She had only gotten fully over that situation two days ago. She would be completely daft to take up with another man. That was the rationale she knew would save her friendship with Ben.

But an hour later, when she walked Ben to the door and he didn't even look like a man who might possibly be thinking about kissing her, Gwen had to remind herself that she was relieved that they'd straightened out their relationship. She absolutely refused to acknowledge the burst of disappointment she felt, because she needed a friend right now more than she needed a confusing courtship.

Chapter Six

"I want ducks."

"Ducks?" Ben echoed incredulously, glancing around the empty bedroom Gwen planned to make into her nursery. Everybody agreed that the walls needed painting. Ben had even decided to replace the ceiling tiles. But no one had said anything about raiding the barnyard. "What in the heck do ducks have to do with babies?"

Gwen laughed with delight, the sound filling Ben with that feeling he had yet to understand or identify. He knew he liked her. And just as he had told her the day after he kissed her, he liked her company. Most of the time he could even convince himself that it was simple loneliness that drew him to her house every day. Other times, like when she laughed, he suspected it was more. But he also suspected that giving his feelings a name would actually add to the confusion of why he was pulled to her house each day, not reduce it.

"Look," she said, opening a binder to display pictures stored in plastic sheet protectors. "This is a model I made from a stencil I have for ducks. The duck is yellow, his rain hat is pink and the raindrops falling all around him are blue. That way, if the baby is a boy, we've covered blue. If the baby is a girl, we've covered pink.''

''And if it's a neutral, you've covered yellow,'' Ben said, stifling a chuckle as he walked over to the bare window to check to see if that, too, needed repair.

''I like it,'' Nathan said, giving the stencil a curious perusal. ''But won't drawing all these ducks take a long time?''

Gwen shook her head. ''Not really. Once the room is painted, we give it a little drying time, then use spray paint over the stencils to create the actual picture. The work goes pretty fast once you get started.''

Pretending to be giving his attention to inspecting the room for other possible defects to which he should attend, Ben covertly listened to Gwen as she taught Nathan. That was another thing about her that he couldn't seem to get out of his mind. It was clear from the way she nurtured Nathan that Gwen was cut out to be a mother. She was homespun, sweet and genuine, yet she was a competent businessperson, very capable of taking care of herself and the baby financially. But more than that, and the thing that really confused him, she had some sort of sexual edge about her that he couldn't quite put his finger on. He was sure that was why he was having the devil's time figuring out her place in his life. If she were only homespun and sweet, he would know how to categorize her. If she were simply sexy and attractive, he would know how to deal with that. But the combination was driving him nuts.

He was happy to have her as a friend, happy to have someone to ''come home to'' every night and share the evening meal. He was also grateful that she was helping him with the burden of steering Nathan's life in the right direction. But he was bewildered about everything else. He'd never had a friend he was attracted to before, and that one little aspect of the situation reared its ugly head at the oddest moments, throwing everything completely off-kilter. There were some times in the past two days when he actually became dizzy and witless from it, and was willing to chuck everything and kiss her again.

If it hadn't been for the fact that Gwen seemed so content not to be kissed, to simply have his friendship, and to keep everything uncomplicated between them, he knew he would have kissed her a hundred times.

Luckily, she did have her wits about her.

Except for the damned ducks.

"The only thing I can't figure out is if I should have them marching in a straight line, like a border on top of the wall, or if I should scatter them all over the walls arbitrarily."

"Oh, dear God, woman, if you've got to have ducks, at least put them in a line. Give them some order and some sense of purpose."

"Or put them in the middle," Nathan suggested, and walked over to the wall. "Make a line of ducks about here," he said, pointing to a spot about shoulder level for the nine-year-old. "That way the baby will be able to see them, too."

The comment didn't make much sense from the perspective of the baby's being able to see them, at least not to Ben, but it once again showed Ben something Gwen must have seen right from the beginning. Nathan had an eye for color, balance and perspective. If Gwen could teach him to pull those things together and use them, Nathan would someday have a wonderful career.

And that was where the mystifying part of this relationship kicked in again. That realization should have brought Ben nothing but a grateful, platonic feeling for her. Instead, it made him want to kiss her again.

"Okay, time for Nathan and me to make our first trip for supplies," Ben said, thankful for all the natural opportunities to get out of the house when he was feeling like this.

But Gwen said, "Just give me five minutes to put on a clean shirt and grab a coat."

Ben shook his head, put his hands on her shoulders and turned her in the direction of the nursery door. "Nathan and I are enough manpower to handle this. Besides, this trip we're only getting generic things like wood, nails and plaster. If we need to buy anything that requires more than carpentry knowledge, we'll be sure to take you along."

"At least let me give you money."

"Are you kidding?" Ben said with a laugh. "I own this house, I pay for the repairs."

Spinning to face him, Gwen said, "But you wouldn't have to redo this room if..."

He silenced her with a finger over her lips and felt the jolt of attraction again. It seemed to spiral from her lips to his finger, down his arm, and radiate to every part of his body. He drew a long breath, determined to ignore it. "The ceiling is outdated. Parts of the wall need repair. The window needs caulking. I would have done it for Satan if he rented from me."

The analogy made her shake her head and turn away from him, obviously unaffected by their physical contact, confirming for Ben that they'd made the right choice in deciding to be only friends. He took Nathan shopping for the things they needed and spent the afternoon teaching him, the same way Ben had seen Gwen teach Nathan. Simply by showing him things as they came up. When they purchased the nails, Ben taught him about nails.

When they scouted the new ceiling tiles, Ben explained the type they would need and why.

All in all it was a very productive afternoon, except that teaching Nathan the way he was, Ben came face-to-face with the other thing that had been bothering him since the night he and Gwen discussed his past: his heritage. The fact that he felt he'd missed out.

He never told Gwen that he felt he didn't fit, but he knew he didn't. At least not in the way that he believed he should. He hadn't had training at a mentor's knee. There were hundreds of things he didn't know about his culture. Kids Nathan's age knew more than Ben about the ceremonies, traditions and rituals of his people. He was at the age where *he* was supposed to be the one sharing, but he had turned away from learning at the first sign of trouble and now he was more in the dark than ever before. Lately, at least since Gwen entered his life, he had actually found himself tempted to question Nathan, to ask questions of a little boy who looked up to him for answers.

It was weird, confusing and wrong. Just like his constant contemplation of kissing Gwen was weird, confusing and wrong.

When they returned to her home later that afternoon, she had homemade chicken soup cooking on the stove. The rich aroma altered the air from something that you breathe to something that you savor. He couldn't stop himself from inhaling and enjoying any more than Nathan could.

"That smells great!" Nathan said, running to the stove for a closer, stronger whiff.

"It was one of my grandmother's specialties," Gwen explained, subtly shifting Nathan a few inches away from the hot pot. Again, mothering without nagging. "I spent summers with her when I was in high school. That's when she taught me to cook. The secret to good chicken soup is parsley and celery.''

"It isn't chicken?" Ben said, laughing.

"Heck no," Gwen said. "That's why a secret stays a secret. If the creators had called this 'parsley, celery soup enhanced by chicken,' then everybody would be making it as delicious as my grandmother. Since it's called chicken soup, people have to guess at the ingredients. Especially since you strain the parsley and celery out of the soup before you serve it. No one guesses all the ingredients correctly, so no one makes it as good as my grandmother did." She grinned mischievously. "Except maybe me, because she told me her secrets."

"Crafty people, those cooks," Ben said. "What time is dinner? I need to store these things in the nursery, but after that I'm free."

"I only need another twenty minutes for noodles—and twenty-five for these rolls," Gwen said, lifting a dish towel to expose actual homemade dinner rolls.

He dropped his nails. "How do you do this?" he asked, incredulous.

She smiled. "Do what?"

Good question. Do what? What exactly was it that she did to make him simultaneously want to pour forth praises from the bottomless pit of respect he was getting for her, and kiss her senseless?

He opted for the easy way out. "How do you find the time to make things from scratch, teach Nathan and do your own work?"

"Spreadsheets," she said simply, and turned around to give her chicken soup a quick stir.

"Spreadsheets?" Ben echoed, baffled. "My accountant has spreadsheets."

"And I have spreadsheets," Gwen said. "I have one that keeps track of housework. One that organizes my work schedule. One that takes Nathan's progress into consideration. One for baby things. Spreadsheets." She paused, then grinned. "Glorified lists," she explained, and went back to her soup.

"Whatever," Ben said, making a quick escape upstairs. He wasted an extra minute or two inspecting the room again, because the truth was he wanted to treasure this time when Gwen and Nathan were downstairs content and happy and he was busy and happy and everything seemed right with the world. Occasions like these might make him see Gwen in ways she didn't want to be seen by him, but they also grounded him into reality. If he were to kiss her again, he would lose all this peace and tranquillity. He would lose this sense of belonging. He would lose something special for Nathan. Only a fool would risk all that for a kiss.

When Ben discovered Gwen had also made thick, chewy homemade noodles for her homemade chicken soup, he pretty much figured he'd died and gone to heaven. Which reinforced his decisions while puttering in the nursery. He didn't want to lose this. Didn't even want to risk it. And one look at Gwen's contented face and he realized she didn't, either.

What they had was absolutely perfect—except that he still wanted to kiss her.

Ben was replacing ceiling tiles a week later when Gwen got the phone call from her cousin Hannah, who had recently opened a day-care center. Hannah had graciously given Gwen all the time and space she needed to get herself organized and oriented, but after over a week of not hearing from Gwen, Hannah had run out of patience. She wanted to know everything Gwen was doing, and the very second Gwen dropped Ben's name, Hannah issued a dinner invitation.

"I'm not sure I can come," Gwen protested, gnawing her bottom lip.

"Why not?" Hannah asked simply.

"Well, I have a standing arrangement with Nathan that he eat dinner with me. I did it originally to get company for myself, because I felt out of sorts in the beginning, but now it's become something like a routine."

"So bring him."

Gwen grimaced. "Well, there's a little more than that to it."

"Like what?" Hannah asked, and Gwen could hear the smile in her voice.

Gwen grimaced again. "Like it started off with Nathan and me eating dinner and Ben coming by to take Nathan home, and pretty soon Ben was joining us for dinner."

"So bring him," Hannah said, and Gwen squeezed her eyes shut. This was exactly what she was afraid of.

"It's not what you think."

"I don't think anything except that you're making friends," Hannah said, and Gwen hoped it was true because she didn't want to have to explain her way out of something she didn't understand herself.

"Jackson will probably appreciate having someone to talk to while I fill you in on local gossip."

Gwen suddenly realized that it wasn't so much local gossip, but information about the local hero that interested her. In the next second, she recognized that her cousin Hannah, a woman very well connected to the community since she watched nearly everybody's children at the day-care center, could fill her in. "What time do you want us there?" Gwen asked, and Hannah burst out laughing.

The conversation with Hannah didn't last more than another minute. Though Gwen was smiling as she hung up the phone, when she turned toward the stairway and heard Ben whistling, the full import of what she had done hit Gwen like a ton of bricks. She had an unusual "friend-ship" with one of the most eligible bachelors in Stork-ville. But she was newly divorced and pregnant with her ex-husband's child, so she couldn't have anything more than that.

If she wasn't careful with how she handled introducing her relationship with Ben to the residents of Storkville, *she* could become the object of that local gossip she was so willing to hear. Not because of Hannah, but because of the people in town who saw her and Ben together. In that instant, she realized it was a good thing that Ben hadn't allowed her to go with him to get the supplies, and even wondered if he hadn't done it on purpose.

With every step Gwen took up the stairs on her way to the nursery to talk with Ben, she felt more and more guilty, realizing she might have let a cat out of the bag that Ben hadn't wanted set free. At the doorway to the nursery, she paused, gathering her courage as she watched him work.

With Nathan in school, Ben was alone, the afternoon sun streaming over him, his dark hair shining in its light. Because of the warmth the bright rays brought into the room, he wore only a white T-shirt and jeans, dispelling any doubts she might have had about what he looked like beneath the vest he seemed to wear all the time. All in all he was the epitome of excellence to her. Not only because he was physically perfect, with his muscled body, thick shiny hair and probing dark eyes, but also because he was innately good. And searching. For what, she wasn't sure yet, but she could tell he was searching, watching everything closely, seeming to question everything he saw, making her long to help him.

But since he hadn't asked for her help, and hadn't even really explained about the quest that kept him coming to her house, watching every move she made with Nathan, and curious about even the simplest things like cooking, Gwen knew he didn't want her help.

"I think I have a bad confession to make," Gwen said from the window, and Ben yelped in pain.

"Ouch! Ouch! Ouch!" he growled, shaking his hand out as it were on fire. "You scared the hell out of me! Never say that to a man with a hammer."

"Sorry," she muttered, and inched into the room.

"What's this big confession?" he asked. "You burn a soufflé? Blow a fuse? Set fire to my porch?"

"If only it were that simple," she said, wringing her hands.

Ben's brain stopped. He'd been thinking about how cute she looked in her checkered maternity top and jeans when her words and her expression finally pierced his foggy thinking and brought him into reality. "What did you do?"

She drew a long breath. "My cousin Hannah invited us to dinner on Friday night and I accepted."

He felt his brows come together in question. "Us? How did she invite *us?*"

"See, I knew I shouldn't have agreed," Gwen said quickly, apologetically. "But it all happened so fast. She asked me to dinner, I told her about Nathan, she told me to bring Nathan and I told her about you. Before I knew it we were all going." She paused, peeked at him. "She'll be disappointed if we don't go."

And he would make it look as if there really was something going on between himself and Gwen if he refused.

If they truly were just friends, and he was convinced that was all they should be, then a simple dinner invitation shouldn't fill anybody with trepidation and/or fear.

"That's fine," he said, then went back to his work to downplay the significance of his easy acquiescence. "In fact, I think we'll have a good time."

He watched her breathe her usual sigh of relief when he said or did anything that confirmed they were only friends and almost cursed. He would sure as hell like to know what this ex-husband of hers looked like, or behaved like to be such an irreplaceable icon in her eyes.

That brought him up short. He knew it wasn't what her ex-husband did *right* that kept Gwen from another relationship. It was what he'd done wrong that had her running scared. She wasn't pining for her lost love. She was scared.

And Ben had to remember that. Because the truth was, he would hurt her, too. He wasn't the kind to settle down. She needed somebody to settle down with her. All that was already on the books and recorded. And he damn well wished he'd stop forgetting it!

"Friends?"

Gwen looked at her cousin Hannah, who had issued the question with such skepticism that Gwen laughed. Four years older than Gwen, Hannah had brown hair with blond highlights and big brown eyes, and was more like a sister to Gwen than a cousin.

"Yes, Hannah, we're only friends. Can't a man and woman be just friends?"

"Not according to the research," Hannah replied caustically.

Gwen laughed again. "Take a look at me, Hannah. I'm

seven-and-a-half months pregnant. I'm not a sex symbol. I couldn't attract a man if I wanted to.''

"Oh," Hannah said, turning to glance at Gwen. "So what you're saying is that things might be different after the baby's born?"

That was territory Gwen didn't care to delve into. She liked Ben too much as a person. Being attracted to him complicated things and risked what they had. So the daydream of changing their relationship once the baby was born, which insistently sneaked into her recent afternoon work time, was not welcome. Hannah mentioning the possibility was equally uninvited. The facts spoke for themselves. She and Ben were friends, on the way to becoming *good* friends. Ben didn't seem to want any more. Given her romantic history, she would be foolish to try for anything more. She couldn't believe she would be so silly as to conjure the daydreams, let alone linger in them.

"I don't want to be anything other than his friend."

Hannah breathed an unexpected sigh of relief. "Well, thank goodness."

"Thank goodness?" Gwen echoed, confused. "I thought you liked this guy."

"I do," Hannah hastily conceded. "Everybody does. But he's just…''

"Just?"

"Just not known for his fidelity."

Gwen stared at her cousin. "He cheats on women?"

Hannah quickly shook her head. "No, it's not that. It's more that he's…''

"A philanderer?"

Hannah shook her head again. "No," she said, then pulled her lower lip beneath her teeth, thinking. "Did you ever hear of serial monogamy?"

Gwen nodded. "Yeah."

"Well, Ben is always faithful when he's in a relationship, but his relationships aren't ever long-term."

"Oh," Gwen said, her heart falling in disappointment, even though she knew it shouldn't. She had no plans for things to go any further between Ben and herself than they already had. So why her heart gave a sudden thud and her stomach did a flip-flop, Gwen didn't know.

"And he's never made a commitment," Hannah continued quietly.

Though inside Gwen felt like weeping, she shrugged. "Really, Hannah, that's none of my business."

Because it wasn't. As Hannah put the finishing touches on her salad and chatted about how lucky she was that the twins in her custody went to bed early and usually slept all night, Gwen reminded herself that none of this could mean anything to her. She had vowed to keep her wits about her and she would. She wasn't in the market for another man. And even after the baby was born, she planned on being too busy mothering her child to get involved with a man—no matter what her silly daydreams were trying to drag her into.

On top of that, there was the whole matter of her exhusband. The pain of rejection. The pain of realizing how wrong she was. No. Absolutely no. She had no fear of getting involved with another man who would ultimately desert her.

"Don't worry about me, Hannah," Gwen told her cousin as she took her hands and squeezed lightly. "Remember Tim? He taught me more lessons than thirty self-help books could have. I'd be a fool to get involved with another man so quickly, and I'd be a double fool to get involved with a man who has a commitment phobia."

Hanna breathed a visible sign of relief. "So I don't have to worry?"

"You don't have to worry. We're friends. He needs somebody. I need somebody. Nathan needs both of us. There is nothing going on beyond that."

"Speaking of Nathan," Hannah said. "Where is he?"

"He couldn't make it. When I called his foster mother she told me that he has a big history report he's been avoiding and she wanted him to spend the evening at home working on it."

Hannah grimaced. "You don't think he's been hiding at your house to get out of it?"

"I'm certain of it," Gwen said with a laugh, taking the bowl of salad to the dining room table. "The kid is nine, and at nine he doesn't see a reason to pay attention to anything he doesn't like."

Following Gwen, Hannah laughed, too. "As proprietor of the local day care, I know exactly what you're saying."

"I think we're about to discover Nathan has the natural ability to become an architect or engineer, but that doesn't mean he can skip history and health. Tomorrow, I'll talk with him about it."

"Talk with who about what?" Jackson said, entering the dining room from the door on the far wall, with Ben on his heels.

"Nathan had to stay behind to do a project tonight," Hannah explained to her husband as she walked up to him and put her arm around his waist. A tall man with dark hair and bright blue eyes, Jackson was perfect for Hannah. "Gwen feels the need to remind him that he's not supposed to put off his homework."

"All little boys put off homework to the last minute," Ben said with a chuckle, taking a seat at the table as Jackson directed him to.

"Including you?" Gwen asked, catching his gaze.

But when their eyes met, though both of them were

laughing about Nathan, something odd happened. Gwen felt the room disappear and felt as if Ben were the only person in the world. From the look in his eyes, Gwen sensed Ben felt it, too. She also felt a click of rightness that what they were doing was exactly what they were supposed to be doing. But she dismissed the episode, relegating it to the knowledge that she and Ben were good for Nathan. *Right* for Nathan. And that's why all this suddenly felt good and right.

But Ben didn't have those same sane thoughts. This feeling of rightness was so new for him that he didn't know how to handle it. Also, being a person of direction and goals, it seemed wrong to ignore it. How was a person to ignore something that constantly called to him? How was a person to ignore something that held the promise of everything he ever wanted?

So he watched her. All through dinner, he watched her make silly conversation with her cousin, watched her in her element, watched her calm and comfortable and relaxed. By the time they were walking back to his truck, he had made up his mind. One kiss was not going to kill either of them and neither did it a commitment make. She wouldn't take it as a promise of a future. They didn't know if they had a future. But they had had a good night, a fun night. Gwen would see this kiss as a seal of closure on a happy night.

He slowly drove his truck onto the gravel driveway that led to her cottage, and silenced the engine. When she reached to open her door, he stopped her by placing his hand on her forearm. "Let me."

Because she was accustomed to him helping her navigate because of her awkwardness, she complied with his request. She let him open her door and lift her down from the high seat of the truck. She even let him unlock her cottage with his keys. Which, for Ben, secured the wonderful sense of rightness that permeated the air. The sense that everything was as it was supposed to be. So, when he reached down, settling his hands at the small of her back to nudge her forward so he could kiss her, it confused him that the movement seemed to shock her.

He pressed his lips to a mouth that felt as if it were opened into a surprised O, and that one little deviation from plan ruined his goal of an uncomplicated, friendly, almost chaste kiss and took them from simple to passionate in about three-and-a-half seconds.

Again, he felt like a man who had tumbled over the edge of everything. Tasting her, touching her, made him forget easy, normal things like breathing and common sense. He liked the way she felt in his arms. He loved the smooth, velvety texture of her skin. He loved the sweetness of her mouth and the silken warmth within. He felt things with her he'd never felt before. Not merely physical things, but emotional things like freedom and safety and need. A need that was so sharp and so real he didn't quite have a way or means to describe it, let alone understand it.

And that was what frightened him.

He broke them apart, and for ten seconds there was nothing but the sound of labored breathing. Then he took a close look into Gwen's eyes, and he saw the fear and knew that *this,* this fear, this apprehension, so readable in her eyes, was the thing that had to keep him in line.

Yet Ben knew it hadn't worked to keep him in line tonight, and now that they both knew that first kiss hadn't been a fluke, he wasn't sure it ever would again.

"I'm going," he said, and took his trembling hands from her shoulders. "I'll bring Nathan by in the morning," he added, then strode away.

The bottom line to this seemed to be that he shouldn't see her again, but he couldn't figure out how to make that happen. Not only did he have to finish her nursery, but for the first time in his life he seemed to be moving toward something right and good. If it weren't for the fact that he knew he frightened Gwen, wild horses wouldn't be able to keep him away.

In the truck, he squeezed his eyes shut, amazed at his insensitivity. He couldn't believe he was thinking of himself, of his needs, when hers were so much more important. Why couldn't he just walk away and stay away as an honorable man should?

Chapter Seven

Gwen didn't even ask why Ben hadn't stopped in to say hello the next morning when he dropped off Nathan, except today she also knew that he wouldn't be coming for lunch that afternoon. If what Hannah told her was correct, Ben wasn't in the market for a commitment. Because she was pregnant, he undoubtedly saw her as a woman who needed a commitment, and in a sense that was true. She wasn't getting involved with another man who would ultimately leave her. Which made their kiss the night before no different from the first one. It was a mistake. Something that never should have happened. But since it kept happening, since they seemed to be drawn to each other, Ben's way of solving the problem was to avoid her.

Confused by her disappointment, because she shouldn't want a relationship with Ben any more than he appeared to want a relationship with her, Gwen decided she needed a bigger diversion than either Nathan or work could provide. Telling her nine-year-old friend that they were going to shake things up a bit with an adventure, she drove them to Hannah's house.

Though Gwen had stayed with Hannah for her first two weeks in Storkville and knew all about the day-care center Hannah ran from her beautiful Victorian home, she was surprised to find that children filled the main room with laughter and noise.

"I didn't know you took kids Saturday mornings," Gwen said as she guided Nathan through the front door and into the fray.

"With Christmas less than four months away, everybody's trying to get extra money by working overtime, especially the shopkeepers."

Gwen laughed. "I suppose."

"And speaking of shopkeepers, here comes one now," Hannah said, reaching out to take the hand of the first of three children walking in around Gwen and Nathan.

Gwen stepped out of the way. "My goodness! The triplets!"

"Aren't they gorgeous!" Hannah said, removing the hat of the little boy, then kissing him soundly on the cheek. "Hello, Lukas."

Three-year-old Lukas shyly looked at the floor.

"These are Molly and Kelly." Hannah introduced the children to Nathan, who stood wide-eyed beside Gwen.

"And this nice lady is their mother, Dana Hewitt." Gwen picked up the introduction for Nathan, pointing out the brunette with the friendly gray eyes. "She manages Bassinets and Booties. It's a store in town where mothers can buy everything they need for their babies. Dana, this is Nathan Eastman. He helps me lift and bend and stretch, since I'm on my own now."

"How do you do," Dana said, extending her hand to shake Nathan's.

Gwen glanced down at her protruding stomach. "It looks like I'll be a customer soon."

"We have some great inventory," Dana said enthusiastically, removing her coat. "I think you'll have a good time just browsing."

"I'm sure I will," Gwen agreed, happy to have something to think about to take her mind off Ben. Darn his hide, anyway, for kissing her! Why did he have to keep confusing their situation?

"Can you stay for coffee?" Hannah asked Dana, and Dana glanced at her watch.

"I have fifteen minutes."

"That's long enough to get my cousin oriented about what she's going to need."

"Actually, I'm doing okay," Gwen began, but Hannah laughed.

"How can you be doing okay, when this is your first baby and you've never actually seen an infant in your entire life?"

Gwen shrugged.

"Have you started your nursery yet?" Dana asked as Hannah led them through the hall to her cheerful kitchen.

"Yes," she said. Because Nathan had integrated himself into the playroom filled with kids and toys, she sat at the table glad to enjoy a few minutes of grown-up conversation. "Ben and Nathan painted. Then Nathan and I stenciled a duck border while Ben replaced the ceiling tiles."

"Ben?" Dana asked curiously.

"Ben Crowe," Hannah supplied helpfully. "He's her landlord."

"Oh," Dana said, but Gwen heard the edge in her voice, the tightness.

Luckily, the sound of Hannah's ten-month-old twins

crying came through the monitor. The little boy and girl had been left on the doorstep of the day-care center with nothing but the clothes on their backs and one worn rattle. While Sheriff Tucker Malone tried to locate their mother, Hannah was granted temporary custody.

"That's my cue," Hannah said, and began to run to the back stairwell. "Gwen, you know where everything is. Serve the coffee, will you?"

"Sure," Gwen said, grateful for the interruption that nicely took them off the subject of Ben.

"Cute kids," Dana said, referring to the twins.

"Adorable. It's a shame that they were abandoned the way they were," Gwen said, and immediately thought of Ben. She knew the pain of abandonment. Though she was an adult, abandoned by her husband, she still knew the feeling, and she couldn't help but wonder how different that pain would be for a child. And how it would affect his relationships for the rest of his life.

"I have my suspicions about the situation," Dana said, but she paused.

Glad to keep the conversation off herself, Gwen said, "What kind of suspicions?"

"I think the baby's mother couldn't handle things alone anymore."

"Probably," Gwen agreed, knowing that the mother of triplets would definitely have a solid opinion on the motive of a mother with twins. "But why drop them in Storkville?" Gwen asked, as Hannah came down the steps carrying one twin on her arm and the other in a carrier hooked over her shoulders.

When Dana didn't answer, only looked at Hannah, Hannah sighed. "We think the mother left the kids here in Storkville because the babies' father is from Storkville."

"Oh," Gwen said, again agreeing with the reasoning.

"Actually," Hannah continued cautiously, "it's even been bantered about that Ben might be the kids' father."

"No way," Gwen said, not even realizing how easily she jumped to his defense. "He was abandoned himself. There is no way he would abandon a child. Look how he's taken to Nathan."

"I didn't say anybody absolutely thought it was him," Hannah immediately said. "I'm just saying, he's a possible contender for fatherhood." She paused, caught Gwen's gaze. "Particularly if the children's mother didn't tell him she was pregnant."

"So, what do you think she's trying to do?" Gwen asked skeptically. "Get the father to guess these are his kids?"

Dana shrugged. "Stranger things have happened," she said, then rose from her seat. "I've got to open the shop, but I'll be back at lunchtime." She glanced at Gwen with a smile. "The store's only open until noon today, so if you feel like browsing, you have to do it early."

Gwen returned her smile. "I may not be by today, but I will stop in sometime soon. I still don't have curtains."

"Well, honey, have I got some ducks to show you," Dana said with a laugh, then made her way back down the hall and to the front door, where she kissed each of her children goodbye. Before any one of them could cry over the loss of his or her mother, Hannah's assistant stood by to shift the child from Dana and deftly return him or her to the play area.

"If it's any consolation, I think you're right about Ben," Hannah said from behind Gwen, and Gwen turned around to face her cousin.

"You do?"

"Sure," Hannah said easily, sliding the first twin into

a high chair. "I think he has too much honor to leave a pregnant woman." Placing the second twin into the matching high chair, she bit her lower lip. "In fact," she said, her voice dropping to almost a whisper, "there are days when I wonder if he isn't the benefactor who anonymously gave me the money to open this day care."

"That does sound like something he'd do," Gwen agreed, obviously relieved that her cousin shared her opinion about Ben.

"I know," Hannah said, "but don't make too much out of my opinion of him, all right? Ben has had a huge impact on this community. The scholarships he funds are a godsend for most of these kids. But on a personal level I stand by what I told you yesterday. I don't think he knows how to make a commitment."

Gwen sighed, knowing it was time to say the words aloud in the hope they would sink into her brain and stop some of her natural instincts toward the man who had befriended her. "I know that's true, Hannah."

"But," Hannah prodded when Gwen picked up her coffee spoon and toyed with it.

"I hate to admit this, but I lied to you last night. I know Ben's not the committing kind, but some days I wish it weren't true," she said, catching Hannah's gaze. "I tell myself he's never going to settle down. I don't think he can. I think being abandoned by his parents and not feeling connected to his people had a huge impact on him."

"But," Hannah prodded again, when Gwen again fell silent.

"But the volume of the little voice in my head keeps getting lower and lower. And some days I'm tempted to turn it off completely."

"Oh, Gwen," Hannah said with a gasp. "Don't fall in love with this guy!"

"Hannah, I'm trying like heck not to, but it is hard. He's at my house every day. We're basically raising Nathan together. And he's fixing my house. He's literally remodeled the room that's going to be my nursery."

Though she expected a stern lecture from her cousin, Hannah surprised her by sagging with relief and affectionately patting her hand. "I think I know what's wrong."

Glad that somebody did, Gwen said, "What is it?"

"You're over seven months pregnant, right?"

Gwen nodded.

"You're in the nesting stage."

"The nesting stage?"

"When a woman gets to be about seven months pregnant, she starts to look for a home for her baby. That's probably why you got so antsy about moving out of my house," she said with a laugh.

"Or it could have been that I didn't want to live with schmaltzy newlyweds," Gwen suggested wryly.

"Do you want to hear this?" Hannah countered, chuckling. "Or do you want to think you're nuts for the next several weeks because you can't seem to stop thinking about a man who isn't good for you?"

"I want to hear this," Gwen said emphatically.

"Okay, you're nesting. You want to make a home for your baby. You found a house and pretty soon you also found another child who needs you, so you took him under your wing because your hormones are telling you that's what you're supposed to do. Mother everyone."

"Hannah, I don't feel motherly toward Ben, if that's what you're thinking."

"No, Ben falls into another category. Look at your life, Gwen," Hannah said insistently. "You got a house and more or less adopted a needy child. Along comes a man who begins making repairs to your cute little cottage, turning it into the home you always wanted, so you feed him. You make him breakfast, lunch and supper, just like a wife, while he does all kinds of husbandly things.'' She paused and smiled at Gwen. ''You are not nuts, you are nesting. It's an instinct. You are doing what comes naturally.''

''So what do I do about this nesting instinct?''

Obviously thinking about her answer, Hannah sighed heavily. ''I don't know. But I think the place to start might be to quit spending so much time with Ben, and for Pete's sake get him to stop doing things around the house.''

Gwen agreed heartily, and even liked Hannah's thinking because it made her feel that she wasn't foolish or stupid, just a victim of nature. It also gave Ben an out, too. She decided he wasn't heartlessly confusing her by kissing her and spending so much time with her, but also a victim of his own instincts. After all, a good, honest, honorable man would feel it was his duty to take care of her.

Satisfied with all that reasoning, she let the subject drop and allowed Nathan to enjoy the company of the other children at the day care for a few hours before she drove him home for lunch. After they ate, knowing that Ben would be too cautious to come to her house until it was time to retrieve Nathan, she suggested to Nathan that they tackle the big project of placing her books in the shelves in her living room. She'd been putting it off because she didn't want to do all the bending and stretching involved, but with Nathan's help she thought the task could be accomplished quickly.

Pleased, Gwen dragged the first box of books from behind her recliner and Nathan began handing them to her. As they worked, she chatted with him about school, reminding him that every subject was important and that he shouldn't ignore projects that don't interest him. Her feelings toward Nathan and his response to her reinforced what Hannah had said. She was mothering Nathan. It all made sense to her now.

They worked companionably, with Nathan bending to get the college textbooks from the box and handing them to Gwen, who lined them up on the shelves. But when he gave her *Black Elk Speaks,* a book she'd been required to read for one of her freshman classes, she stopped dead in her tracks.

She knew the book shouldn't have inspired the eerie feeling that washed over her, since it had been among her possessions for years, but it did. Not because she'd picked up the life story of the Sioux holy man at this precise second, but because she'd forgotten everything she'd learned when she read the book. If she hadn't spoken with Hannah that morning about nesting instincts, she might have been tempted to read the book again to see if she would find something that would help Ben find a connection to the Sioux. But since she'd talked to Hannah and knew she was fighting emotions ingrained in nature, she didn't think it wise to link herself to Ben any more than she already was.

But when Ben came to get Nathan and he looked tired and drawn, Gwen knew she couldn't chalk that up to Ben fighting his natural instincts toward her. She had always known something troubled him. He'd admitted he felt awkward about his past. She had a book in her bookcase that could open the door for her to understand him, maybe help him.

Wouldn't it be awfully selfish of her to ignore that?

The following night when Ben stopped to check up on her, she met him at the door with a book. He knew that she knew he had no intention of going inside and he hoped the book wasn't a ploy to get him to break the promises he'd made to himself. "What's this?"

"It's a book I had to read in college," Gwen said, then nervously licked her lips. "I found it yesterday, when Nathan and I were putting my books in the bookcase," she added, directing him to look at the cottage's built-in bookcases, which were now filled to capacity, because, Ben suspected, she wanted him to recognize she hadn't fabricated this story. "It's very interesting. I read it again last night. It's got some good stuff in it."

Ben stared at the book. He remembered reading it years ago. He remembered liking it. "Thank you," he said self-consciously.

"You're welcome," Gwen said, giving him a cautious smile. "We can talk about it, if you would like, after you read it."

Not quite sure what else to do, because he couldn't say for certain he would read it again, Ben only nodded.

"I also wanted to tell you that I understand a little more about what's happening between us," she said.

Because she was so awkward, so hesitant, Ben could see it was costing her to be so bold, and his heart froze with fear. If she'd given him a gift to soften him up for when she proposed they actually start a relationship, he didn't have a clue what he'd say. Half of him knew he was a bad risk, particularly to someone vulnerable, and that half knew he should stay the hell away from her. The other half wanted a relationship with her so badly he had to fight himself to stay away from her house.

"Hannah explained to me that pregnant women get nesting instincts," she said, glancing down at her hands. "I took what she said and factored in some male instincts and I think that you're more or less going through the same thing. You might not be my baby's father, but because you're my landlord, in some ways I think you feel duty-bound to take care of me.''

He wasn't sure where she was going with this conversation, but since he couldn't argue with what she'd said, Ben conceded the point with another brief nod.

''So, my instincts to make a home are colliding with your instincts to take care of a woman you perceive to be in trouble, and we're making a big mess out of things.''

He smiled. If he took all his sex drives out of the equation, that basically summed it up. ''I guess.''

''Ben, it's obvious to me that you don't want a relationship. But the truth is whether or not you want a relationship with me is irrelevant. I *can't* have a relationship. With these hormones I'm not really in control. It would be foolish of me to get involved with anyone before I have this baby.''

He looked at the book, looked at her. ''What are you saying?''

''I'm saying that we're friends. All I want to be is friends. I don't want you to feel you have to hide from me anymore.''

That wasn't precisely what he was doing. He was running from himself and his own urges, not from hers. Lucky thing, too, since it appeared her feelings for him were hormone-related. Not real, growing emotions, only substitute love for the love she should have been showering on her baby's father right now. If it hadn't hurt to hear her admit it, it might have been funny. But it did hurt. It stung.

Of course, she'd found excuses for his behavior, too. Any normal man would feel honor-bound to help her. In spite of the fact that she continually reminded him she didn't need his help, because he was her landlord he did notice things that needed to be fixed. Because he was her neighbor, and he knew no one drove on this road but people going to his ranch, he did feel it was something like his responsibility to check on her periodically. If you eliminated all the male-female issues, even his behavior could be explained away. There was no reason for anyone to be embarrassed or hurt.

He drew a long breath. He supposed the book could be construed as a peace offering. Something less personal for them to talk about. An avenue to establish a normal relationship between them. Because he did feel the need to look in on her and help her, and they were also connected because of Nathan, they needed a way to shift their focus.

"I see what you're saying."

She peeked at him. "Really?" she asked hopefully.

"Really," he said, more firmly this time. "I'm sorry I keep stepping over the line."

"We've both stepped over the line," Gwen insisted. "But now that we know the line is there, we'll both be more careful," she said, opening her door a little farther, a silent invitation that he could step in.

A short debate took place in his brain. In the end he decided that she was right. They couldn't avoid each other indefinitely, and they were both smart enough to ignore a few wayward hormones.

A few days later when Ben suddenly became hesitant and formal around her again, it first insulted Gwen. But soon she realized he wasn't so much hesitant as uncomfortable.

As long as he had something to repair in her house, he was okay, but once the nursery was done, the banisters were repaired or replaced and every window had been caulked, he couldn't relax in her home anymore. Particularly not at mealtime.

From the things both Nathan and Hannah had told her about Ben's place in the community, Gwen deduced that might be because he was the one accustomed to doing the favors, rather than receiving them. She thought it was sad that he could do so much for others, but not feel comfortable with simple kindnesses extended to him. And she also decided it was time somebody turned the tables on Ben Crowe. It was time somebody was good to him. For no reason or purpose, especially not as payback for a favor received, just because he was a nice guy who deserved to be treated well.

So when he arrived on Sunday night, doing his usual check on her after returning Nathan to the reservation, Gwen was ready.

"Hi," she said, when she opened her door to him.

"Hi," he said but he didn't put his hat on the peg or remove his coat. "Just making one more check to be sure you're okay."

"I'm fine." She smiled. "How are you?"

That made him frown. "What do you mean, how am I?"

She shrugged, effortlessly leading him to her kitchen table just by walking in that direction. She took a seat and he automatically sat across from her. "You've been a little quiet over the past two days." She paused to look at him. "Since you've run out of work to do here."

"I've had things on my mind."

She leaned her elbow on a sunny yellow place mat and her chin on her closed fist. "Like what? Did something come up again with your accountant?"

It surprised him that she remembered, but he tried not to make too much out of that. "He's gone."

She grimaced. "I guess you did have a little bit more trouble with him, then."

"A bit," Ben agreed, unsuccessfully stifling a grin.

The conversation died, but before Ben had a chance to even think about leaving, Gwen said, "Can I get you something? Coffee? Tea? Maybe some ice cream or a cookie?"

"Are you trying to make me fat?" Ben asked suddenly, knowing that she fed him so much and so well he was becoming spoiled by it.

She laughed. "Heck, no!" she said, but from the way the words came out Ben got a strange jolt of recognition. In a backhanded way, she'd just told him she liked the way he looked. She liked his body.

He felt the a shiver of awareness and wondered if he wasn't giving more meaning to her tone than she'd intended because that's what he wanted to hear. It was odd and difficult to be at her house three or four times a day with nothing to do but look at her, watch her, talk with her. Not because he sensed he shouldn't be there, but because he sensed he should. Some days he wanted to hold her and tell her everything would be okay if they would just take this slowly. But he would remind himself of his own dubious past and the fact that she'd come right out and told him she didn't want a relationship with him, and he could stomp that idea out before he acted on it. But tonight she didn't look disinterested. Tonight she looked very interested and very beautiful. And half his strong argument for staying away from her disappeared like snowflakes in the Sahara.

Almost thanking God for his dubious past, which protected her when she didn't seem to want to protect herself, he rose. "Well, if everything's okay here, I'm going to head on home."

"Okay," she said pleasantly, and rose, too. "I'll see you in the morning."

"Not for breakfast," he said, deciding that on the spot. Since the day she'd given him the book, she had been too darned nice to him, and it was starting to wear him down and make him think there was more behind her behavior than hormones and instincts. Though he knew she didn't want to be seen in the context of being his lover, and though he could think of a thousand and one reasons why he didn't want to see her in the context of being his lover, that image kept jumping to his mind. He was starting to take her smiles and touches and kindnesses as affirmations that she liked him, too, and he knew he couldn't. She wasn't right for him. He wasn't right for her. Period. Yet her being nice to him made him think that wasn't true.

So he showed up on her doorstep after ten the next morning with new tiles for her bathroom. If she was going to spoil him, he was retaliating. No one got the better of Ben Crowe when it came to giving. But more than that, because he was back to doing repair work, every nice thing she did for him could be considered her way of showing her appreciation for his hard work and he didn't have to wonder about her motives anymore.

Plus, fixing her cottage gave him the excuse he needed to be around her without having to consider *his* ulterior motives. He was only here because she was alone and it wasn't right for a woman who was so far advanced in her pregnancy to be alone in a house out in the country. His motives didn't go any deeper than that. He wasn't here because he liked her, though he did. He wasn't here because his own house was suddenly big, empty and lonely, though it was. If he focused on the fact that he was here because he didn't want her to be alone, and she was being nice to him because he was making repairs on her cottage, he didn't have to take his thoughts about either one of their motives any further than that.

But when she didn't even ask if he wanted lunch, simply let him work until two o'clock in the afternoon, Ben tiptoed downstairs and peered around the banister at her. She was at the kitchen table, reading a cookbook. For a person he had worried was spoiling him, she didn't look the slightest bit concerned that she'd forgotten his lunch.

When she saw him, she smiled. "Hungry?"

"Starved," he said, and hesitantly made his way into the kitchen. "What are you doing?"

She shrugged. "Reading recipes."

"Are you making something special for dinner?" he asked.

She nodded. "Always. I love to cook."

Her answer brought him up short, forcing him to acknowledge that she wasn't cooking special things for him, or even treating him special, she was merely indulging her own penchant for cooking. If that was true, then, really, he had nothing to worry about from her. All he had to do was keep *himself* in line and they would be okay.

He relaxed, made himself a sandwich and disappeared upstairs again. He wondered if he hadn't merely convinced himself that she was interested in him because of his infantile obsession of not letting anyone do more for him than he did for them, but told himself these tiles were worn and had needed replacing. In fact, maybe it was time to check some other areas of the cottage to see what else might have fallen into disrepair.

Comfortable that Gwen's feelings were nothing more than overactive hormones and his feelings were controllable as long as he had work to do, Ben jogged up the steps and made the quick right turn into her bedroom. He didn't feel uneasy poking and prodding, because he was looking for excuses to stay around her because she needed him. She was lonely, awkward and about to have a child. Duty and honor compelled him to be at her house as much as possible.

So when he found himself peeking at her dresser when he was supposed to be checking the woodwork behind it, he decided his eyes had only wandered. When he lost the battle to prevent himself from opening one of the perfumes in the cluster on her vanity and taking a whiff, he considered it nothing but normal curiosity.

If he sniffed one too many containers, read all the inscriptions on her knickknacks and keepsakes, and smiled at her choice of bed linen, he told himself it wasn't because he was interested in Gwen and unable to control himself. Those things simply got in his way as he investigated the structural state of her bedroom. He was not going to fall in love with this woman—he wasn't! Not only was he an unreliable suitor, but she was too vulnerable to take the risk.

Satisfied with that rationale, and also that the walls and woodwork of her bedroom were in good shape, he pulled open the closet door only to be confronted by something that completely shocked him. Two rows of business suits.

He didn't know why that should surprise him. She told him she had a career before she came to Storkville. He supposed that what caught his attention was that he actually recognized the clean lines of the designer, because these were the kinds of suits that Julie had worn. A simple career woman wouldn't buy the suits of Julie's designer. Only a filthy rich, or incredibly image-conscious woman would. Since Ben knew Gwen wasn't a woman who tried to make people believe she was someone she wasn't, his only remaining option was that Gwen was rich....

Or he was wrong. The truth was he could be dead

wrong about these suits. What the hell did he know about fashion designers, anyway? A smart man would close the doors and walk away and forget all this.

But he couldn't.

Telling himself he was being ridiculous, Ben nonetheless pulled out one of Gwen's suit jackets and rummaged for the label. He read the name and his mouth fell open. Not because he knew what one of these suits cost, but because of what the cost of one of these suits meant.

Shocked, irritated that he hadn't seen this coming, Ben sat on her bed. As if there weren't enough differences to complicate his relationship with Gwen, she had to come from the same social circle—at least social sphere—as the woman who left him.

The woman who would live with him, but wouldn't marry him, because he was Sioux.

He ran his hand down his face and told himself that this didn't mean anything, couldn't mean anything, but he knew it did. Because finding those suits had paralyzed him with an emotion that right now defied description, he had to ask himself why. Why was this was such devastating news if he really didn't care about Gwen as anything other than a friend?

Was he falling for her?

Was he only kidding himself to continue to pretend that he wasn't?

And if he was beginning to fall in love with this woman, if she'd sneaked by his defenses already, how the heck was he going to prevent himself from falling completely?

Ben didn't know the answers to those questions, but he did know one thing. He wasn't going to let himself fall. He vowed four years ago that he would never set himself up to be hurt again, and that was one vow he intended to keep.

Chapter Eight

The following morning when Hannah called Gwen and asked her to come in to help out at the day care because she was shorthanded since her assistant had called off sick, Gwen hesitated. She wondered if she wouldn't give Ben the wrong impression if she wasn't home the morning after he'd run out of her house as if his boots were on fire.

She'd spend the entire day subtly ignoring him so he would see that their relationship wasn't going over any boundaries, and that they really could be friends. She actually thought he'd gotten the message that he could be relaxed and comfortable with her, but from the way he'd left, it seemed her trick had backfired. Instead of reassuring him, she had somehow made him even more uneasy than he was before.

What she wanted to do was give him the one gift no one else seemed to be able to give him: acceptance without the expectation of something in return. But it seemed she ignored him so well he felt unwelcome in her home.

Now she was afraid that if she wasn't at her house this morning it would cement the idea that she had been avoiding him the day before, he would stop coming to the cottage altogether, and she would never get the chance to help him sort out his past.

Which was her real bottom-line goal. She finally realized that the thing that drew her to Ben was that he was as confused about his life as she had been about hers. Having found the answers to her own problems, she felt more than a little bit like an expert. If Ben could just give her two or three weeks of honest conversation she knew she could help him settle his issues. But to get those two weeks, she was going to have to gain his trust. And she would never gain his trust if he couldn't depend on her to be home when she was supposed to be.

Because Hannah sounded frazzled since even Gertie and Emma who frequently volunteered at the daycare center couldn't spare any time, Gwen knew she didn't have a choice and she arrived at the day-care center at the same time Ben probably arrived at her front door and found her gone. She hoped the note she left would sufficiently explain that her leaving had been a necessity. But she couldn't really pacify him since she didn't know why he'd run out on her the night before. Confused and edgy, she stepped on Hannah's front porch at the same moment that Hannah opened her front door.

"Are you okay?" Hannah asked, pulling Gwen inside.

"I'm great, fine, wonderful," Gwen said, then removed her light jacket and hung it in the hall closet. "Hi, Dana," she added, seeing the triplets' mother on the floor in front of a small brightly colored plastic table, obviously giving her children some last-minute attention before she left for work. A single mom, Dana appeared to take advantage of every opportunity she had to spend time with her children.

"Hi, Gwen," Dana happily responded. "You're looking big," she said with a laugh.

Gwen grimaced. "I know. I seem to be growing with leaps and bounds."

"That's what happens in your last two months," Hannah said, then turned to walk down the hall. "I have a schedule in the kitchen of the kids' activities for the day and a list of comings and goings."

"Comings and goings?" Gwen asked curiously.

"Yeah," Hannah said, chuckling. "I have parents who pick up their kids for lunch, and parents who only need day care for a few hours in the morning and parents who don't need day care until after lunch. Some days I feel like I should have installed a revolving door. Without Penny Sue we're going to need this list."

"Right," Gwen said as Hannah made her way back to the kitchen.

"So how are you?" Dana asked seriously, rising from her seat on the colorful rug on the floor, all three of her children gathered around her.

"Not as tired as I used to be."

"Oh, I see the nesting instinct is kicking in," Dana said with a laugh. "If you've finished your nursery, expect yourself to want to start washing windows, scrubbing walls and replacing everything that even appears to be slightly damaged, because your instincts will be screaming that everything needs to be perfect for the baby."

Gwen laughed. "My instincts are going to be greatly disappointed. Not only did I scrub everything before I moved into the cottage, but Ben's replaced everything that could possibly need replacing. He even put in new bathroom tiles and I swear they weren't faded, let alone chipped or cracked."

As she said the last, Hannah walked into the day-care

room. Hearing what Gwen had said, she frowned. "Ben's still hanging around?"

"He's not hanging around," Gwen said with a chuckle. "He's fixing things."

"He's getting the nesting instinct, too," Dana suggested, catching Hannah's gaze.

"Now, you two just stop it," Gwen said incredulously. "First of all, I know both of your intentions are good, but I've just been hurt and I'm not stupid. I'm not going to get involved with a man who's not good for me. Second, Ben isn't the town criminal. Actually, from the way I hear things, he's very good to everyone. But listen to the way you talk about him."

"We don't mean to make the guy sound like a creep, because he isn't," Hannah said.

"No, he isn't," Dana quickly agreed.

"But you can't stop us from worrying about you," Hannah said, placing her arm around Gwen's shoulders. "Your emotions aren't exactly stable. One of these mornings you're going to wake up in love with that guy and you're going to be sorry."

Gwen stiffened. "I don't think so."

"I do," Hannah insisted.

Obviously uncomfortable, Dana glanced down at her triplets, then at the front door. "I guess I better go."

"Oh, Dana, I'm sorry," Hannah said, and immediately reached down to lift Kelly. "Come on, little Kelly Belly," she said, then tickled the little girl's tummy. "It's cookie time."

"Yeah, it's cookie time," Gwen agreed, reaching down for the hands of Lukas and Molly. "Where do we go for cookie time?" she asked, smiling at Hannah.

Though Hannah returned Gwen's smile, her look was equally filled with concern. When Dana was gone and the triplets were settled, Gwen caught Hannah's arm and led her out to the foyer for privacy.

"Hannah, please don't worry about me."

"I have to," Hannah said with a sigh. "I see something in your face when you talk about him and I think you're going to get hurt."

"What you see is concern. Or maybe compassion for the little boy who was abandoned. He needs someone to listen to him and guide him, and I want to be that person," Gwen said quietly. "Not just for him but for me. Over the past weeks I've realized that having someone to think about instead of dwelling on my own troubles has been very good for me. I have no plans to fall in love with him, but, honestly, Hannah, it's been a welcome diversion to have someone else to be concerned about for a change."

"You couldn't be concerned about Nathan?" Hannah said solemnly.

Gwen smiled. "Of course I'm concerned about Nathan! I'm concerned about you! I worry about everybody. Heck, I even worry about Dana raising these three kids alone and I hardly know her. In another week or two I'll be offering her unsolicited advice. But for now, I seem to need to help Ben figure out his past. It's a simple, platonic, uncomplicated gesture of friendship. And that's all."

Because Hannah seemed so edgy, Gwen decided she had to move a little more quickly in her bridge-building with Ben, and she realized she had the perfect avenue to get him talking in *Black Elk Speaks*.

She couldn't believe the reminiscence of one man could give such a clear accounting of a culture, but Black Elk's stories did exactly that. She knew that if Ben had read the book, he would have different feelings than he had before and she also believed he would want to share them. Once he began talking, he would discover that Gwen was a good listener and he would realize that if he needed someone with whom to sort through his past, she was that person.

So, when Ben returned to check her locks after driving Nathan to the reservation, and not only didn't stay an extra second, he also didn't speak—except to grunt unintelligible responses to her chipper questions about *Black Elk Speaks*—Gwen began to suspect he still wasn't over the issue that had troubled him the night before. She was all set to ask him about it, but he never gave her the chance. He bolted from her cottage the very second he was sure all the locks were secure.

The next day when he didn't arrive at her house until it was time for dinner, and then didn't speak during the entire meal, Gwen knew something serious was troubling him. When she again couldn't get him to spend an extra second in her home when he arrived for his nightly ritual of checking the locks on all the windows and doors, she almost panicked, until another thought struck her. Because she kept trying to get him to talk about *Black Elk Speaks,* she considered that he might not have read the book and didn't want to disappoint her.

But the following night when he announced that he wouldn't be back to check on her because he was taking Nathan shopping after dinner and didn't know what time he would be back, Gwen was completely confounded.

First, it looked like her plan was not going to work. She was never going to get Ben to open up to her so she could help him understand his past. Second, she was a woman—a professional shopper—yet no one had asked her along on this trip. She didn't know whether to be insulted or mad, then decided to be neither, but to imagine they hadn't asked her because they weren't sure she would want to go. That being the case, she would invite herself along.

"I could use a shopping trip myself."

Nathan looked uncomfortable. Ben downright squirmed.

Gwen's eyes narrowed. "Why don't you want me to go?"

"It's a guy thing," Ben said, trying to sound casual, but Gwen didn't buy it. She'd seen his initial squirming.

"What kind of guy thing?"

"We're going for...nails," Ben said, as if he'd just thought the last part up.

Gwen turned to Nathan. "You don't have to go nail shopping," she said ingeniously. "You can stay here with me. I'll take you back to the reservation."

"I want to go shopping!" Nathan cried, his bright brown eyes growing huge and luminous. He faced Ben. "Ben, I want to go shopping."

"All right, look," Ben said, turning to Gwen with a heavy sigh. "Nate and I want to buy your baby a present, okay? So we want to go ourselves."

Pleasantly surprised and also touched, Gwen held back tears. Ben might be avoiding her, but he cared about her, almost confirming that the most likely reason he kept running out of her house was that she kept trying to get him to talk about a book he hadn't yet read.

"That's so sweet," she said, then dabbed at her eyes only to discover they were overflowing with tears. "But it's also impractical. Nathan, I don't pay you money every week for you to turn around and spend it on me. I wanted you to spend that money on yourself."

She began to rise from her seat to get a tissue, but Ben

caught her wrist and stopped her. His dark eyes narrowed at her, he said, "What money?"

Not really seeing the harm in telling him, Gwen sighed. "I pay Nathan twenty dollars a week for helping me. It's no big deal."

But when Ben's eyes narrowed even further and he turned that thunderous gaze on Nathan, Nathan squirmed in his chair. "She pays you money to visit her?"

"Oh, for heaven's sake," Gwen said, jumping in, saving Nathan from Ben's unreasonable reaction. "It's only twenty dollars a week. And he does at least twenty dollars a week in work for me."

"Well, that's good, because I pay him fifty dollars a week. So, he's getting paid seventy dollars a week to do twenty dollars' worth of work."

Nathan appeared sufficiently caught and guilt-stricken, but Gwen seared Ben with a look that would have cowed a lesser man. "What would you pay him fifty dollars a week for?" But even as she said the words, she realized what had happened and she gasped. "You pay him to baby-sit me, don't you?"

"It's not like that," Ben said, dismissing her concerns and fixing his attention on Nathan, who turned his big soulful brown eyes on Gwen as if begging for mercy. "Why didn't you tell me that Mrs. Parker was paying you?"

Nathan hung his head. "I knew you would stop paying me if you knew Gwen was."

"I see."

"Well, I'm glad you see," Gwen said, not about to let her questions go unnoticed, or Ben Crowe get off scot-free in this episode. "Because I sure as hell do not see why *you* would pay Nathan for something that concerns me. When did this start, anyway?"

As if only realizing that he had been busted every bit as much as Nathan had been, Ben faced Gwen. "Oh-oh," he said, the look in his eyes going from furious to guilt-ridden with the speed of light.

"Oh-oh is right," she said, then fell to her seat in disbelief. "I can't believe this. You're paying him to stay with me."

"It's not what you think. I didn't realize the cottage needed as much repair as it did, and that I'd be here every day," Ben explained rationally. "So, I enlisted Nathan's help to make sure someone stopped in regularly to check on you. I couldn't very well take back my promise to pay Nathan once our situation mushroomed into me fixing the cottage and us eating almost every meal together because we're friends," he said, accenting the word *friends* with his deep, solemn voice and catching her hand.

"That's just it," she said. "We are friends. You should have told me." She yanked her hand away from Ben's and combed her fingers through her hair. "This amazes me. Here I thought I was the one person in Storkville who didn't take you for granted and the whole time you're paying someone to baby-sit me."

"That's not how it is," Ben insisted.

"The point is, I wanted to do things for you without you returning the favor. I just wanted to love you. Free of commitment and complications. Free of strings. Free of you feeling that you have to even the score."

Now it was Ben's turn to be stunned. "What did you say?" he asked quietly.

"I said I wanted to do things for you without you feeling that you had to even the score," she angrily recounted. "And instead…"

Ben interrupted her. "No. Before that. Before you said

you wanted to do things for me without me evening the score. What did you say before that?''

"She said she loved you," Nathan replied, easily filling in the blank because, Ben could see, he was happy to have the spotlight taken off him. But Ben also saw Gwen's face turn ashen.

"I didn't say that," she said, gasping.

But she had said it and in the sudden silence of her usually busy kitchen, Ben could tell from the expression on her face that she was remembering having said it. Not only did she remember saying it, but it shocked her.

Which didn't surprise Ben one bit. Her admission shocked the hell out of him, too. For thirty seconds, he let the thought that she loved him soak into his weary soul. A quick cinema of their potential future showed in his brain. The fun, the laughter, the love. All the wonderful things a man wanted and received from a woman he loved tempted him, and he knew that at that moment he could reach out and take them.

But he also knew she would change her mind. He'd seen the suits. He knew the signs. He wasn't going to be a fool twice in his lifetime. He wouldn't set himself up for a river of pain.

"Nathan, how about running upstairs to the nursery and making sure all my tools are put in the right boxes?" he said quietly.

Grateful for the opportunity for escape, Nathan jumped from his seat. "Sure."

When the sound of his footfalls on the stairway faded into nothing, Ben again took Gwen's hand. "I know you're embarrassed by what you said, but it doesn't have to be a disaster."

She wouldn't look at him. "I just told you that I love you," she said softly, staring at their entwined fingers.

"And I know darned well that you don't love me. I'd say that has *disaster* written all over it."

"It could," Ben agreed, holding on to his control by only a thread. He wanted to believe she loved him, because with only the slightest push he could love her, too. But he refused, absolutely refused to step over that line because it wouldn't work and he wasn't going to put them in the position of trying to make it work. She might think she loved him now, but even she admitted she was overwhelmed with hormones and instincts. Once the baby was born she would feel differently.

And then one of them or both of them would end up hurt.

"Gwen," he said softly, and hooked his finger under her chin, forcing her to look at him. "I've seen the designer labels in your closet. You downplay your past, but it's clear where you come from."

He paused long enough to give her a chance to reply. When she didn't, he said, "You're here to have your baby because it's safe. You needed a refuge from your ex-husband and you found one. Part of you genuinely believes you're staying."

"I am staying," she whispered, desperately searching his eyes.

He nearly cursed at the need that whipped through him, because the desire to hold her, to comfort her was so strong he almost couldn't control it, but he did. He didn't curse and he didn't lose his courage, his restraint. He had to do this.

"We come from two different worlds and yours is a world I don't fit into. You might enjoy a year or two of total privacy and seclusion with your baby, but can you assure me that when your child is school age you won't decide he or she needs private schooling?"

"I don't understand what that has to do with anything," Gwen began, but Ben stopped her.

"Look around you, Gwen. Storkville is a nice place for a rich woman to visit, but it's not a place you're going to want to live permanently. And I simply do not fit into your world." He rose, called to Nathan, then turned to her again. "I won't even try."

"You know, even ignoring the fact that you're wrong about me wanting to leave Storkville, the bottom line to what you're saying is that you think I'm a snob."

He shook his head. "Snobbery has nothing to do with it. It's roots. You *should* want the best for your child."

Gwen lifted her chin. "I think the best is right here in Storkville. Good people. Open spaces. Fresh air. Those are the things a child really needs."

This time Ben did curse, albeit under his breath. She didn't know how tempted he was to believe her. But she also didn't know he'd been down this road before and was painfully aware that he couldn't hang his heart on something as fragile as another person's current whim.

"I think you're wrong," he said, then grabbed his hat and ushered Nathan out the door. He didn't even say goodbye. He couldn't. It took everything he had not to haul her into his arms and kiss the stricken look from her delicate face.

But when he was gone, Gwen sat at the table, stunned and confused. She'd spilled her heart out to him, and he'd politely handed it back. It was shocking enough to realize she loved him, worse to have admitted it in such an unexpected way, and achingly overwhelming to realize it was all for nothing.

He didn't love her.

When she laid her head on her folded arms to cry, she knew hormones had nothing to do with it.

* * *

This time when Gwen went to the day care, it truly was for comfort and advice. Because Dana had been in on most of the discussions Hannah and Gwen had shared about Ben, and because Dana seemed to be as caring a person as Hannah, Gwen wasn't surprised when she followed them back to Hannah's kitchen.

"Okay, what happened?" Hannah asked without preamble.

"Oh, Hannah, you were right. I let everything get out of hand and now I'm so confused I can't think."

"What happened?" Hannah asked again, settling Gwen on a chair. Dana got her a cup of tea.

"I did the stupidest thing, and the truth is I didn't even mean to do it."

"What did you do?" Hannah asked patiently.

Gwen grimaced. Now that her tears were gone and she was able to look at everything objectively, she felt embarrassed to admit this to her cousin but knew she had to. "Somehow...in conversation, mind you...I told Ben that I did some of the things I did for him because I loved him. What I meant to say was that I did the things for him that I did because I wanted to be good to him, but somehow everything got all screwed up."

"No, right here is where you're getting screwed up," Hannah said, pointing to Gwen's head. "You really are falling in love with this guy, and you're trying to convince yourself that you're not because you know it's wrong."

"I know it's wrong. Boy, now more than ever I know it's wrong," Gwen said, then sipped the tea Dana had given her. "But I just feel awful for him, Hannah. He seems so alone."

"It's how he chooses to live," Dana reminded Gwen from her position of leaning against the kitchen counter.

"But why? I don't understand," Gwen insisted. "He loves people. He is the most wonderful, generous person I know. Why does he want to keep to himself?"

"Who knows?" Hannah said, raising her hands as if defeated.

"Do you know the reason he gave for not wanting to have anything to do with me?" Gwen said, agitated now.

Hannah shook her head.

"He said it's my roots. That I'll want to go back to the kind of life Tim and I had...."

"Or the kind of life you had with your parents," Hannah speculated hesitantly. "You know, we've all thought about this from the perspective of you and Tim and the baby, but none of us ever took this down to the next level."

"What level is that?" Dana asked curiously.

"Gwen's parents are very wealthy," Hannah said simply. "Gwen doesn't understand how wealthy because she's accustomed to ignoring the lap of luxury, but she's from a place most of us only dream about."

Dana laughed, but Gwen scowled at her. "Are you saying Ben might not like me because my parents are from McLean, Virginia?"

"No, I'm saying he might be super cautious because your parents live in a mansion...along the Potomac," Hannah corrected.

"Oh, right," Dana said through a sigh, as if just figuring something out for herself. "I get it now," she said, glancing at Hannah. "You're thinking about Julie, aren't you?"

Hannah nodded.

"What?" Gwen asked, looking from Hannah to Dana.

"The last relationship that Ben had that looked like it might have been on the road to being long-term was with an Omaha socialite by the name of Julie. She came here to do some charity work and naturally bumped into Ben. They started dating and divided their time between his ranch and Omaha.''

"And?'' Gwen prodded when Hannah stopped talking and glanced at Dana again.

"And everybody thought he dumped her,'' Dana supplied. "Isn't that odd. We all just assumed he dumped her because he never made commitments. But what if it was the other way around?''

"What if what was the other way around?'' Gwen asked, again looking from Hannah to Dana.

"If it was, the women of this community are going to be kicking themselves for discouraging their sisters, friends and *cousins* from going after him,'' Dana said, giving Hannah a pointed look.

"Because he might not be the villain here,'' Hannah said with a groan. "Oh, why didn't we see this sooner?''

"Maybe we weren't supposed to,'' Dana said logically. "I mean, the guy holds his cards so close to the vest. He's very proud. He might not have wanted us to see he was the one who got hurt.''

The rest of the conversation was lost on Gwen, particularly since Dana and Hannah somehow veered off in a completely different direction once they decided Ben had taken a beating from Julie while most of the community had painted *him* as the bad guy.

Hannah and Dana took a second or two to feel guilty for pinning the blame in the wrong place, but for Gwen the conversation had an entirely different result. Not only did Ben's being hurt perfectly explain his behavior and hesitancy, it also opened the door for her to fix things.

She loved him. It had taken an entire day and an admission from her subconscious, but the realization had finally sunk in. And she wasn't losing him without a fight.

Chapter Nine

Nathan arrived after school as he always did and Gwen cheerfully greeted him at the door. Seeing that she was happy obviously relieved the little boy, causing Gwen to recognize that she not only had to work out her relationship with Ben, she had to sort through some things with Nathan, too.

Because it hurt him when she and Ben fought, somehow Gwen had to put their friendship into perspective for him. Otherwise, he would never survive if she tried to force Ben to admit he loved her and Ben rejected her.

When she had him settled at the kitchen table with a glass of milk and two cookies, she said, "Nathan, you do understand that no matter what happens, you and I will always be friends?"

He nodded. "Yeah."

His flippant answer made Gwen feel he didn't fully grasp what she had said, so she elaborated. "I guess what I'm trying to say is that what happens between Ben and me shouldn't have any impact on our friendship."

This time when Nathan nodded, he caught her gaze and Gwen felt he had understood her.

He ate a bite of cookie, drank a swig of milk, then said, "Ben took away twenty dollars."

"Excuse me?" Gwen asked, stifling a laugh. She was pretty sure she knew what was coming but wanted to hear Nathan explain it.

"He said that I was double-dipping and that wasn't fair."

"Being paid by two people to do the same job really isn't fair," Gwen agreed, gently siding with Ben because he was right and Nathan needed to accept that. But he also needed to see that even though Gwen and Ben might disagree about some things, there were other things, more important things, about which they agreed.

"So, he said that since you were paying me twenty dollars every week, he would subtract twenty dollars every week from what he owed me, but I was still getting at least fifty dollars, which was what he promised me. Though it was from both of you, not just from him."

"That sounds fair," Gwen said, nudging Nathan to acquiesce to Ben's decision.

He shrugged. "I guess."

"Ben's a fair guy," Gwen said.

Nathan shrugged again. "I guess," he said, sounding more positive this time, and Gwen let the subject drop, convinced that Nathan understood.

Because the truth was, Ben was a fair man. She had initially been attracted to him because he was handsome, but she had fallen in love with him because he was fair—as honest and honorable and fair as they come. And his friendship was as important to Nathan's growth as Gwen's was. If Gwen's plan failed, she didn't want Nathan to feel he had to choose between the two of them.

However, when Ben arrived to retrieve Nathan that night at six, he hardly behaved like the fair guy Gwen credited him with being. He walked in her door and started giving orders.

"Let's go, Nate."

"But we didn't eat dinner," the little boy protested, grabbing his coat.

"You can get something at your foster parents'." He looked at Gwen. "Gwen, I'm not going to be eating with you anymore," he stated as if he'd practiced this speech a hundred times. "And if you want Nathan to eat with you, he has to be done before six when I come by to pick him up."

Because Gwen hadn't expected Ben's mood or his sharp tone of voice, she only nodded, too surprised by his gruffness to speak. Equally affected, Nathan shoved his arms into the sleeves of his jacket as he scurried over to the open door by which Ben stood. He ducked around Ben and was scrambling off the porch before Gwen even had a chance to say goodbye.

Hand on the doorknob, Ben drew a long breath. "Actually, I won't be back at all. If you have a problem with something here at the cottage, just leave a message with my housekeeper."

Lips pressed together to hide their trembling, because he sounded so cold, heartless and final, Gwen nodded again. But when he was gone, she refused to give in to the tears. She loved him, darn it. *Loved him.* If he thought avoiding her would cause her to abandon her plan of forcing him to admit he loved her, too, he had another think coming.

"Just tell him we never talked about *Black Elk Speaks.*"

As Gwen made her request, she watched the old woman who had answered the door raise her eyebrows in question. Because Talking Dove wore a lapel pin with her name on it and an apron, Gwen suspected she was Ben's housekeeper. But even though it appeared Talking Dove would have loved to ask a question or two, she said nothing, only nodded and walked away to get Ben.

Gwen would have loved to ask a question or two herself before Talking Dove shuffled off, but she knew better than to pry any further into Ben's life than she already had via town gossip. She felt uncomfortable that she knew about Julie from Hannah and Dana. She didn't want to hear anything else that didn't come directly from Ben.

As she waited for Talking Dove to return, Gwen looked around the grand entrance to Ben's enormous house and held back a sigh of appreciation. Though the place was sparsely decorated, it appeared to have been built to be enjoyed. An airy cathedral ceiling invited you inside. Walls paneled with warm, comfortable wood held a few colorful Native American artifacts. But the leather sofa and chair arranged by a cold stone fireplace, and chilly brass lamps and brass-and-glass end tables snuffed out any welcome made by the natural materials of the structure.

"Gwen?" Ben said, coming down a long corridor from the back of the house. "Is everything okay?"

Not knowing what kind of reaction to expect, Gwen nearly breathed a sigh of relief when he came bounding toward her with a concerned expression on his face.

"I gave you *Black Elk Speaks* so we could talk about it. It wasn't a free gift without strings. I'm curious about your culture. So, since I'm curious and need your help, I also brought you fried chicken."

Ben ran his hand along the back of his neck and said, "Let's talk in the den."

He led her along a hall barren of pictures, decorations or personal touches of any sort and into a den that looked more used than the living room but not more comfortable. Black leather furniture was so shiny and stiff it might have never been sat upon. The huge desk was littered with papers, but gleamed as if still new. The white rug didn't have a smudge or a footprint.

"Is your bedroom this clean?"

She expected him to laugh at her comment, instead his eyes flared just long enough for Gwen to realize her suspicions were correct. He couldn't connect her and his bedroom without his mind wandering into unwanted directions. He liked her. Heck, he'd said it enough times himself. Now all she had to do was prove to him that she was dependable, trustworthy and not going to leave him, and he could admit he loved her, too.

Not such a big deal to a woman with a solid plan.

"I have a housekeeper. That's why everything is always clean."

"You must cringe when you come to my house," she said, setting her basket of chicken on his desk and walking around to inspect the place.

"I love your house," he said, his voice almost a whisper.

She faced him with a grin. "I know, so do I. That cottage is wonderful."

"It was deserted before you," Ben contradicted, his voice turning cool and dispassionate. He took his seat at the desk. "You made that house a home. But I don't have all day, Gwen. What is it you want?"

"I wanted to talk about *Black Elk Speaks*. Since you

aren't going to be coming to my house anymore, I realized I'd have to come to yours.''

"With chicken?"

She smiled again. "I'm always hungry."

He sighed heavily, but peeked under the lid of her basket. "Did you make these rolls?" he asked, but the question almost came out as an accusation.

"Guilty."

"Damn it."

"Aw, come on, Ben. It's not a crime for me to be a good cook. And it's not a crime for you to like my cooking...." She paused, caught his gaze. "Or my company. I'm lonely. I miss you." She looked around his cool den. "And don't even try to say you don't miss me."

"Last night was the first night I haven't eaten supper with you in over two weeks," he reminded her. "I haven't had time to miss you."

"Sure you have," Gwen cheerfully disagreed, then stripped off her jacket and took the seat in front of his desk. "So what did you think of the book?"

"I love that book," he said.

Obviously realizing he wasn't getting rid of her and too polite to insult her, he handed her one of the paper plates she'd stashed in the basket, then offered her the container of chicken first. She snagged a leg. He took a breast and a thigh.

"When I read those stories, I feel like I'm living them."

"I had the same feeling," Gwen agreed. His grudging acceptance of her in his home wasn't a declaration of love, or even friendship, but it was a start. "My favorite was the story about the brave who wanted to marry the daughter of the grumpy chief and ended up stealing a herd of horses. But in the end, he won the girl."

"Only after spending the day in a hollowed-out log because he was naked and painted black and white and most of the tribe thought he was an evil spirit."

Gwen couldn't help it, she laughed. "It's a good story."

"Yeah," Ben agreed. "It's a great story." He caught her gaze. "And this is good chicken."

"And you missed me."

A few seconds ticked off the clock as Gwen waited to see if he would be honest. Finally, he said, "And I missed you."

"And you'll come back?"

"Gwen..."

"Ben, I'm sorry for what I said, not because I didn't mean it but because I don't think you're ready to hear it...."

"I'm not..."

"I know. You're not the kind of guy to settle down," she conceded blithely. "But I'm not looking for someone to settle down with me." She paused, then did what she knew she had to do. "But I'm close to my last month of pregnancy and I need someone to be with me. Hannah can't come because she's got the day care. Nathan's in school the majority of the day." She held his gaze. "I have no one, Ben. I need you."

She could see from the look on his face that she'd struck the nerve she intended to strike. He closed his eyes for a second, then said, "You're right. I'm being selfish. I won't let you down."

She would have felt guilty for playing on his honor the way she had, but the truth was, all she wanted was time. He had come so close so many times to admitting he was falling in love with her that she knew it was only a matter of time. And with her request that he stay with her until the baby was born, she had bought them more than a month.

She kept the conversation light and friendly after that, and pretended not to notice when he didn't kiss her good-bye at her car door. Things like that would come later. For now, it was good enough that he could admit he missed her, and good enough that he was willing to resume their friendship, albeit cautiously.

When he walked into her house in time to help set the table for dinner that night, it took everything Gwen had not to smirk with smug satisfaction. It took everything she had not to kiss him hello since she was the one leading this relationship forward. But she didn't, mostly because of Nathan.

The wide-eyed little boy looked from her to Ben as if he didn't know what to expect. Gwen didn't know how to explain this situation to him, and she was starting to wonder if it was a bad thing to have him involved at all. The problem was he was already involved and he would stay involved because there was no way to get him out without hurting him. But there was also no way to explain to a nine-year-old that he should prepare for the fact that all this could be gone any day.

Particularly since Gwen was having trouble understanding it herself. They all liked one another. They all needed one another. They all enjoyed sharing the evening meal and basically keeping company with one another. So none of them really "wanted" this to end.

She acknowledged that Ben had been hurt, but she had been hurt and she got over it, then she found her new happiness with Ben, in his goodness and his strength. She knew that if Ben would just take that last step and trust her, he would find his new happiness with her. But he wouldn't take that step, and it confused her. So she knew Nathan had to be even more bewildered than she was.

"How was school today, Nathan?" she asked when they sat down to eat.

He shrugged. "It was okay. My teacher wants to talk with you, though."

"With me?" Gwen asked, confused.

"Yeah, she said something needs to be done about my math grade."

Gwen watched as Ben nearly choked on a bite of meat loaf, but though Ben thought the situation funny, Gwen's apprehensions hitched a notch. If Nathan's teacher needed to talk with someone about his math grade, it should be Nathan's foster mother, not Gwen. Could she and Ben have confused Nathan to the point that he was looking at them as his guardians because he was starting to see them as a family?

"Since you easily taught me perspective and stuff," Nathan continued, "she thinks I should be getting better math grades than I'm getting, and she thinks that if you would show her how you're teaching me, she could probably help me get that grade up."

Gwen almost breathed a sigh of relief. "I'll be happy to speak with her," she said, glad that her suspicions were wrong. But in that second, she glanced at Ben, and saw him watching her. Not in the way a man watches a woman he loves, but in the way a man watches a person he doesn't trust, and she knew he was evaluating her general trustworthiness through her dealings with Nathan.

It wasn't the first time she felt Ben was assessing her character through her behavior with Nathan, and though judging a person's integrity by how they treated others was ordinarily a standard operating procedure, tonight it all felt wrong. Off sync. Her gut instinct that she and Ben had confused Nathan wouldn't go away, and she decided she would have to speak with Nathan's foster mother.

Which wouldn't actually solve the problem. Eating dinner, she couldn't see how she and Ben could keep the little boy in their lives without confusing him even more, or worse, without hurting him. If she pushed Ben into trying a relationship and they failed, Nathan would suffer as much as they would. If they succeeded and ended up together, as a couple, would he feel lost and alone? Or even rejected? They had pulled him into their little drama rather effortlessly, witlessly, and in the end he would be an innocent victim.

When Ben returned from taking Nathan to the reservation that night, Gwen asked him what he thought.

"Nathan's been tagging along with me for a year and a half," Ben said as he made his usual inspection of her windows and doors. "He's not suddenly going to get the wrong impression now."

"But things are different with me," Gwen insisted. "I have him here almost every day. I give him chores. I feed him. I teach him." She paused, bit her lower lip as she looked up at Ben who was at her front door, preparing to leave. "I have a really bad feeling about this."

"What you have are hormones running wild through your system," Ben insisted with a chuckle. "You feel too much about everything."

"Now you sound like Hannah."

"Because Hannah's right," Ben said, pulling her into his arms. God help him, but he was tired of fighting this.

And he had also come up with a rational excuse that sanctioned the special privileges he couldn't resist. He decided that since she had only a little over a month left in her pregnancy, there was no danger that they would cross that one forbidden line. No matter how much she tempted him, they would never make love. Because they couldn't cross that line, he had solid protection for his heart, and since she seemed so willing to let him into her life, then he was staying. But if he was staying, he also planned to enjoy himself. If she wanted to play house with him, then he would play.

But she luxuriated in the warmth of his arms only for a few seconds before she stepped out and stepped back.

"Your heart is too soft," he said, looking at her curiously, wondering if he had misinterpreted her. Maybe she didn't like him in the way he thought she liked him. Maybe she really did simply want someone to check on her every day until the baby was born.

"Even when I'm not pregnant my heart is this soft, Ben," she insisted, failing to keep the worry out of her voice. "I have such a bad feeling about this."

Her pulling away confused him, almost angered him because it was more emotional than physical. She had brought him back into this relationship, and he had one slim month to enjoy it. But now that he had come around to her way of thinking, she seemed to have already changed her mind.

"I don't know why," Ben said cautiously. "You're the best thing that ever happened to that boy."

"That's just it. I can't be the best thing that ever happened to Nathan...."

"Why?" he asked, piercing her with a look when he realized why he felt so suspicious. It wasn't because she was pulling away from him, but because she had stopped any progress in her relationship with Nathan. An honorable woman, she couldn't commit to Nathan because deep down inside she knew she wouldn't always be here for him. "Are you planning to leave?"

She held his gaze, her hazel eyes intent and serious, but

also full of love. The quick shift of the expression in her eyes took them from talking about Nathan, to talking about him…about them.

"You know I'm not."

Her simple statement relieved him so much that Ben knew he was already in way over his head with this woman. He wondered if he was only kidding himself by thinking that he could be around her, hug her, kiss her and take care of her, and keep his heart. Looking at her, seeing the love shining in her beautiful eyes, he almost forgot why he would want to, but he didn't forget. He wished he was wrong, but he didn't forget.

"You know, if you keep saying that, I'm going to start believing it." He tried to pack his voice with warning, but she only smiled at him.

"That's the point," Gwen whispered, and this time when Ben pulled her closer, she didn't shift away.

He bent his head and kissed her, and lost himself to the velvety softness of her mouth and the way she felt so right in his arms. He could have kissed her all night—he *would* have kissed her all night—except he knew she was tired, and he also respected that line, the wonderful line that was going to save their sanity. He wanted to make love to her so badly he ached with it. But he also knew they couldn't. In fact, she was too vulnerable to make any kind of choice right now and he had to be man enough, strong enough, to keep them from doing anything she would regret when her baby was born.

He broke the kiss and she walked with him to her front door. When he turned to say goodbye, he again found himself drowning in the promise shining in those beautiful eyes of hers.

He swallowed. "Good night."

"Good night, Ben," she said, stretching to her tiptoes and kissing him lightly.

It was a sweet gesture, Ben admitted, but darn it, how could she not realize what she did to him? He cupped her cheek with his hand, marveling at the differences in their skin tones and the velvet softness of her cheek up against the roughened callouses of his palms, but before he did something dangerous like kiss her again, he pivoted away.

Gwen caught his hand and turned him to face her again. "Hey, everything is going to turn out okay. You'll see."

"How is it you can always read what I'm thinking?"

She shrugged. "I'm psychic."

Her silly answer made him laugh and he rubbed his hand across the back of his neck. "What you are is driving me nuts."

At first he thought she might argue with him, but she smiled and said, "Thanks."

"You're welcome," Ben said with another laugh, not quite sure where to take the conversation from here. He wanted to kiss her and hug her and maybe even keep her in his life forever, but he knew he wasn't going to. And every time he kissed her, it only made the inevitable that much more difficult to face. Which meant the gestures of affection had to stop.

"I do want to be here for you." He paused, drew in a long, life-sustaining breath, then made the admission that he hoped would give her some perspective of what he was feeling. "But the problem is I want you. I find you very attractive and very sexy."

At her skeptical look he chuckled. "You don't think you have great legs?"

Her face colored and Ben couldn't help it, he pulled her into his arms to hug her. "Oh, Gwen."

But he suddenly remembered the conversation about

Nathan that had taken them to this point, and he knew that the hugs and kisses he was enjoying so much right now would ultimately be his undoing. Though he knew she believed she would stay—at least she did right now, at this minute—he also recognized a subconscious holding back that he would bet Gwen didn't even see. She wasn't exactly bailing out on Nathan, simply being cautious. And though that was commendable in a way, it was also a very telling thing. She wasn't as secure in her feelings about Storkville as she claimed, or she wouldn't worry about Nathan using her as a contact person for school. Hell, he'd been Nathan's constant companion for almost a year and a half. And never once had it occurred to him to be careful about his dealings with the boy. The kid needed company. He needed to think people cared about him. That's all he wanted from Gwen. A little bit of reassurance that she cared. And she was uncomfortable giving it.

"Gwen, the hugs and the kisses have got to stop," he said, then pulled away from her. "It isn't that I don't enjoy them," he explained, confused when her reaction was to continue to smile at him. "I enjoy them too much."

She said, "Okay," and didn't seem too annoyed or upset, which normally would have puzzled Ben, but he wasn't looking a gift horse in the mouth.

Glad that he was keeping his wits about him in this relationship, Ben said a quick goodbye then strode to his truck. Never in his entire life had he been glad he couldn't make love to a woman he wanted so desperately, he ached with it. But he was glad now. Because if he made love to her, he knew he would be lost, and when she had the baby he knew she would be gone.

And he refused to let her take his heart with her when she went.

Chapter Ten

Ben talking about his feelings, albeit to try to talk himself out of them, convinced Gwen she was on the verge of getting him to admit he loved her, and she scrambled the next day to think of something fantastic to make for dinner.

When Nathan arrived at the cottage and he didn't have a hint of a suggestion, they jumped into her car and took a trip to the supermarket looking for something unusual, something wonderful. She bought the items she would need to prepare manicotti, not even thinking that she had never served Italian food before and Ben might not like it.

But when he arrived that evening and sniffed the air as if he'd just entered heaven, Gwen sagged with relief.

Unfortunately, she couldn't unsag. Once she sat down to eat, she realized she had been running around all day and she was exhausted. Afraid to have Ben see that doing her illustrations, keeping up the cottage and making dinner for three people was starting to wear on her, she didn't say anything and began to help Ben and Nathan clean the kitchen. But when she dropped a glass and it shattered into a million pieces, she burst into tears.

"Okay," Ben said, directing her toward the living room. "What happened?"

"It just slipped," she said, sobbing uncontrollably.

"I wasn't talking about the glass," he soothed. "It's a darned glass and it doesn't matter. I was talking about you. You look exhausted."

"I am exhausted."

"But you didn't tell me," he complained. "And I'm the one who is supposed to be caring for you." Though he had been helping her to the sofa, he changed his mind when they reached the bottom of the steps. "I'll tell you what. Why don't you go upstairs and get yourself ready for bed?"

"It's only seven o'clock," she protested weakly.

"I know," Ben said, holding her waist as he walked her up the steps. "I'll run Nathan home, then I'll come back and you and I can play rummy on your bed."

She gave him a watery smile. "That sounds like fun."

"Yeah, it does," he agreed, feeling that he was stepping hip-deep into trouble again.

But the second he guided her into her bedroom and his gaze collided with her closet door, Ben lost all his apprehension. He remembered the suits, which reminded him of Julie, which reminded him that Gwen was off limits. Not only did she come from a background which would someday call her home, but she knew it. Otherwise, she wouldn't have a problem with befriending Nathan. It would come naturally. He didn't begrudge her the right to go home. In fact, in some ways he commended her for being careful with Nathan. And Ben knew as long as he remembered all this, he didn't have anything to worry about. Particularly since he had put their relationship into perspective for both of them the night before.

"Is she going to be okay?" Nathan asked anxiously when Ben came down the steps and entered the kitchen again.

"Sure, she's going to be fine."

"She didn't look fine."

"Nate, she's only tired," Ben explained comfortingly. "Grab your coat so I can take you home." Nathan nodded and scrambled to do as he was told. "I'll bet by the time I get back to check on her she'll be sound asleep."

But she wasn't. When Ben returned, Gwen was wide-eyed and alert.

"I thought you would be sound asleep," he said, entering her bedroom.

She sighed. "Tell me about it. I was so exhausted I thought I was going to die on the spot. I didn't even think I'd make it through a quick shower and sliding into a nightgown. But the minute my head hit the pillow my eyes popped open and I didn't feel the slightest bit sleepy. You bring the cards?"

"Yeah, I have some," he said, producing them from the pocket of his denim vest and tossing them to her on the bed, where she leaned on pillows propped against the headboard.

After a few seconds of glancing around, he kicked off his boots, slipped off his vest and tossed his Stetson to an available chair. As he dealt the cards, he cautiously sat on the far corner of her bed.

"Long day?" she asked quietly.

He nodded. "Some are longer than others."

"Ever buy that horse you once told me you were going to buy?"

He nodded. "Bought four."

The conversation came to an abrupt halt and Gwen despaired of ever getting it started again. But the oddest thing happened, after a few minutes of playing cards, Ben stretched out on the bottom of her bed. She relaxed against her pillows. A nice, easy rhythm developed between the cards and the players and she realized they didn't need conversation.

Sinking into her pillows, she listened to the snap and shuffle of the cards and then suddenly, unexpectedly, she felt all her energy disappear. Like air released from a balloon, she felt her strength and stamina desert her.

"Oh-oh," she said, then she yawned.

Panicked, Ben glanced up at her. "What 'oh-oh'?"

She yawned again. "I'm just tired."

"Oh," he said, obviously relieved. "Good. That's good," he said, scooping up the cards and returning them to their cardboard box. Still propped against her pillows, Gwen closed her eyes. She almost didn't have the strength to slide down in bed.

"You need help?"

She smiled. "No, I'm just sort of enjoying this."

She felt his weight as he sat on the bed again. "Enjoying what?" he asked curiously.

Hearing the genuine interest in his voice, Gwen opened her eyes. "Did you ever get so tired that relaxing feels like heaven?"

He smiled at her. "Yeah, I guess."

"Well, that happens a lot when you're pregnant. You get so hungry food tastes better, so tired that your bed feels more wonderful and so grouchy that the kindness of any human being toward you seems like a gift from God."

Enjoying the moment, she closed her eyes again.

"It was the best of times, it was the worst of times," Ben said with a chuckle. "My foster mother used to say that we needed difficulties to help us to recognize when we've got it good."

That made her giggle. "I can see the wisdom in that."

"She said a lot of really smart things."

For this, Gwen opened her eyes again. "Really?"

"Yeah," Ben said sadly.

"You miss her, don't you?"

"Of course."

"Do you ever visit?"

"Often."

"How long were you with her?"

"Basically, she and her husband raised me. I think that if my mother hadn't been alive, they might have adopted me."

"That's nice," Gwen said, then she yawned.

Ben rose from the bed. "I better go," he said, but Gwen caught his hand.

"No, stay," she said, careful to keep the pleading out of her voice because she wasn't desperate for his company, only happy to have it. "I like hearing about your past."

He snorted a laugh. "What there is of it," he said, then sat on her bed again.

But she removed one of the pillows from behind her head and patted the spot beside her. "Get comfortable," she said, then drew them into the conversation again. "You had as much past as anybody else."

"Not really," he said, tentatively stretching out beside her. "You know other people have things like family history that I don't have."

"Couldn't you adopt the traditions of your foster parents?"

He shook his head. "I would feel I was abandoning my roots." He paused, caught her gaze. "They're not Native American."

She shrugged. "So what?"

"So I felt like I would have been leaving my people behind if I had adopted the traditions of Irish Catholics."

Gwen smiled. "You're not the leprechaun type."

"I don't think so."

"So why haven't you been a little quicker to learn about your own people?" Gwen asked, then shifted until she was able to rest her head on his shoulder.

Feeling very comfortable, and also very glad that she was happy and resting, Ben put his arm around her shoulders and nestled her against his side. "I'm not just a slow learner, I'm actually a very cautious person."

"No kidding."

"And I wasn't sure how far involved I wanted to be." He wouldn't tell her that was because being Sioux had cost him the love of his life. At this point, it was still hard to admit it to himself. But tonight instead of being hurt and confused about losing someone because of who he was, he was suddenly more angry with Julie for being a bigot. He nestled Gwen closer to his side and allowed his fingers to stray to her hair.

"That's why you give money for scholarships, rather than actually mentoring the kids."

"Probably," Ben said, feeling things he'd never felt before. For the first time in his life, it wasn't odd or unusual to be Sioux. It was just who he was. Neither good nor bad, just who he was.

"I would be really curious if I were you," Gwen said, her voice soft and tired again. He felt her swallow and heard her long intake of breath as if she were fighting sleep. "My great-great-grandparents on both my mother's and my father's sides of the family were immigrants. I could trace my family tree back to the dinosaurs if I wanted to, my people were so proud of who they were."

"You're not proud of them?"

"Oh, I'm proud of them," Gwen assured him, trying to figure out how to explain that she hadn't fit into her wealthy family where stock options not best friends or little league were average dinner topics. She didn't want him to form a bad opinion of her parents because she didn't have one. She had simply wanted a different life-style. "I'm very proud, but I wanted more out of life than the family business. I didn't look for a new home here in Storkville because my parents didn't hug me when I had a problem. I went looking for somewhere I would fit. I just wanted to fit."

"Yeah," Ben agreed, remembering how he'd been welcomed at the reservation without question, without qualm. He remembered being so quickly and so easily accepted, he didn't trust it.

"We should go to the reservation together," Gwen suggested sleepily. "You already know who you are, now it's time to find out who you come from. It doesn't mean you have to change. It's just a wonderful thing to understand your roots."

"I guess," he said, then realized she was asleep.

But even though she had been tripping over the edge of slumber, what she said had great significance and Ben thought about it. All of it. Not merely what she said, but how she said it, and why she would come up with such things. It was no darned wonder he liked her. Not only was she soft and cuddly, but she had a great deal of common sense.

He gazed down at her angelic face and for several seconds allowed himself the luxury he could not have when she was awake. He simply looked at her. He studied the shade of her peaches-and-cream complexion, then gave in to the urge to run his finger along the slope of her cheek. She was the softest person he had ever touched. Her skin was like warm velvet. Lured by the smooth perfection, he trailed his finger along her jaw and down her neck. Marveling at her softness and yet impressed with her strength.

She snuggled into him more tightly and Ben shifted to make her comfortable. Though she was bundled in a flannel nightgown and covered with a blanket and chenille spread, he could still see the shape of her stomach and spent a minute peering at that, too. Having been in her company the past six weeks, he fully understood how a person could be multidimensional. She was Gwen, a woman, an artist who could support herself, a homemaker, a housekeeper who could take care of herself, and a mother. But she was also a friend to Nathan and a friend to him. She amazed him.

Tired himself, he put his head back against the pillow-padded headboard and closed his eyes. She didn't have a clue how she tempted him. She didn't have a clue how much he wanted what she was offering. She didn't have a clue how hard it was to remember that he'd tried this once before and it didn't work. No matter what she said now when the time was right she would leave, and he would want her to leave. He would want her to have the best out of life. The best for her and the best for her child. He was not the best.

But for now he was here, he was holding her and that was good enough.

He awakened some time in the middle of the night and slid Gwen down off the headboard. Comfortable and warm, more asleep than awake, he didn't even consider that he should leave and, instead, lay down beside her, drawing her to him. She inhaled a long, satisfied breath and he drifted back to sleep again.

But in the morning, his eyes sprang open as if someone had touched him with a hot branding iron. He glanced down and Gwen was peeking up at him.

"Hi."

He cleared his throat. "Hi."

"I guess you fell asleep," she said, indicating his clothes.

He ran his hand down his face, trying to get fully awake. "I guess I did." He could see from the look on her face that she was making much more of this than she should and realized if he didn't stop making mistakes like this all the good decisions he had made the last night he kissed her would be meaningless. He quickly slid his arms from beneath her and swung his legs off the bed. Panic surged through him. Not for himself, but for her. He didn't want to hurt *her*.

He could accept her hurting him when she left after the baby was born, but he could not accept himself hurting her.

No matter how difficult it was over these next few weeks, he would not give her the wrong impression, or put her into a position she would regret when the baby was born.

Because of the way Ben left her that morning, Gwen knew it was doubly important to make a great dinner. But not only did she fail to find a food that tickled her fancy in her cupboards, she struck out at the grocery store, too. By the time they returned to the cottage Gwen barely had time to get macaroni and cheese in the oven. There would be no homemade rolls. They would have no salad or fresh vegetables. The best she could do was store-bought cole slaw and frozen peas.

When Ben arrived, she was on the verge of tears and Nathan was sitting at the kitchen table, his elbow on a place mat, his chin on his closed fist, staring at her.

"Are you all right?" Ben asked immediately. He strode to the stove and caught her by the shoulders.

"I'm fine," she said tightly, refusing to lose this battle. "I only made macaroni and cheese, though. It was all I had time for."

He grimaced. "I hate macaroni and cheese. I'll just get something when I go home."

The fear that shot through her almost took her breath away. "No. No. We'll find something," she insisted.

He shook his head. "You'll do nothing of the sort. You will sit."

She drew a long breath. "I'm fine."

"No, you're not," Ben contradicted, and directed her to a chair. "I'll put your dinner on the table. You just relax." He paused and smiled at Nathan. "Nate, how about getting Gwen a glass of milk or something."

"I can do it myself," Gwen said, and bounced from her chair, fear pumping through her. She was failing him. She was failing herself, and she was going to lose everything.

That thought weakened her knees, because the last time she had that thought she was with Tim. For two weeks after discovering he didn't want their baby, she'd run around trying to make everything perfect for him so that he would change his mind....

Gwen froze. The fear that had been pumping through her was replaced by a hot surge of emotion she couldn't define or describe. She had run herself ragged trying to keep Tim, now she was doing the same thing to keep Ben. It hadn't worked then. So why was she doing it now?

As Nathan ate his dinner, Gwen toyed with her food. She calmed herself by thinking that these were two different situations and two different men. Tim expected her to cater to him. Ben most certainly did not. Tim had rejected her efforts and always had her jumping through another hoop. Thoughts of that kind of behavior wouldn't even enter Ben's head.

Unfortunately, there was a startling common denominator here. One she couldn't avoid or ignore. In both cases she had been trying to get a man to love her.

And after Tim, Gwen had sworn she would never do that again. If a man didn't come to her of his own volition, then she didn't want him.

Nathan finished eating and Ben directed him to get his coat. She knew she'd been silent and probably confusing during dinner, but she couldn't stop the litany running through her brain. She couldn't believe she was repeating the biggest mistake of her life. At least if she hadn't catered to Tim, she could have left with a modicum of dignity. And if she didn't stop catering to Ben, she would lose all the confidence and strength she'd built since she'd moved to Storkville.

"I'm taking Nathan home now," Ben said, capturing Gwen's attention. "You look tired, but don't go to bed right away, let me come back and check on you."

If Ben had made a suggestion like that that afternoon, Gwen would have been in seventh heaven, thinking of getting private time with him. Now she felt nothing but foolish. And angry. How could she have put herself in this kind of position with a man again?

"I don't want you to come back," Gwen said suddenly, the words startling her as much as Ben and Nathan.

"I'm coming back," Ben said, then maneuvered Nathan out the door and onto the porch. "I'll be right with you, Nate," he said cheerfully, then faced Gwen again. "You look like hell. I'm coming back."

But Gwen shook her head. Never in her life had she felt so stupid, so blind. "I don't want you to come back. In fact," she said, catching his gaze, "I don't want you to come here at all. I want you and Nathan to go back to doing whatever it was you did together before I entered the picture."

"Look, I know you're upset about Nathan. I know you didn't want him using your name with his teacher. But I will call his foster mother and his teacher and talk to both of them, if you'd like, to let them know your place in Nathan's life. He's confused, that's all." Ben ran his hand along the back of his neck. "Hell, Gwen, we're all confused."

But Gwen wasn't confused. She knew exactly what was happening because she had lived it. Only this time she wasn't an innocent victim. If she had fallen in love with a man who didn't love her, it was her own darned fault. And there was only one way to handle it.

"Ben, do you love me?" she asked suddenly into a kitchen that had grown quiet and almost eerie.

"Gwen, this isn't the time to..."

"Do you, right at this very second, love me?" she asked insistently.

He shook his head. "I'm not going to answer that."

"Actually, I think you just did. If you can't say it, then you don't feel it."

He made a move to protest, but she stopped him with a quick wave of her hand. "This is really very simple, Ben. You either love me or you don't. You're either committed to me or you're not."

"I am committed to you. I'm committed to help you get through this pregnancy...."

She stopped him with another wave of her hand. "That's not good enough. I want to hear you say that you love me. Whether you intended to or not, that's the position you put me in a few days ago. I had to decide almost on the spot that I loved you enough that I would never leave Storkville."

"I never..."

"Yes, you did. And I told you I would never leave. In a way I committed myself to you. Now I'm only asking you to return the favor. If you can't, I don't want you to come back. I don't want to find myself jumping through hoops to try to win anybody's love. I won't go through that again."

Chapter Eleven

Furious, confused, Ben turned to walk out of Gwen's house and almost stepped on Nathan, who was standing on the porch, just beyond the doorway in which he and Gwen had argued.

"Let's go," he gruffly commanded, but Nathan only swallowed hard.

"Aw, come on, Nate," he coaxed, quickly closing the door so Gwen wouldn't hear. His first instinct when Gwen started backing him into a corner was to think that her hormones had kicked up again. But when she mentioned her ex-husband, Ben knew that wasn't true. He was being pushed because of the mistakes made by her previous lover, and he refused, absolutely refused, to make the commitment that would be a disaster.

He managed to get Nate into his truck without any more hassle and was greatly relieved until the little boy turned his big brown eyes on him and said, "She doesn't want us back."

"Looks like," Ben said flippantly, not sure how to explain this problem to a nine-year-old. In the end, he chose not to. There would be plenty of opportunities in the future to tell Nathan the truth, and right now Ben was simply too angry to be kind in his explanation. For everybody's sanity, he opted to tease Nathan right now and explain later. "You're only asking because you don't want to lose your fifty bucks."

"I don't care about the money," Nathan mumbled, and Ben laughed.

"Hey, you better care about the money. You still owe me twenty dollars for your share of the music box we bought."

"I'll get it from Nina," Nathan said, referring to his foster mother, Nina Whitefeather.

"That wasn't the deal," Ben said firmly. "The deal was you would pay me back with money you earned from me. Tomorrow I'll talk with Jake, my foreman. I'm sure we can find something for you to do on the ranch."

"I want to go to Gwen's."

"Gwen doesn't want us," Ben said softly, furious at the way that stung. She'd pulled him in. She had done everything in her power to get him in her life and keep him in her life, then she turned the tables as if he'd somehow done something to provoke her. "She doesn't want us and we have to respect her wishes."

"I want my tablet and pencils," Nate said petulantly. "She said they were mine."

"I'll buy you new ones."

"Then I'll owe you more money."

"No, you won't!" Ben said, almost as angry with Nathan as he was with Gwen. Did everybody in his life have to push him into a corner today? "I'll buy them for you as a gift."

"A gift for what?"

"A gift for being quiet for the rest of the way home," Ben said, but the minute the words were out of his mouth he regretted them. He felt as if he were taking his anger with Gwen out on Nathan, but knew that wasn't true. For the past year and a half every time he turned around, Nathan was on his heels. He had been more than patient, he had been kind and generous with the boy, and just like Gwen it looked like Nathan was throwing Ben's generosity back in his face.

Even though he was angry, Ben drew a long breath and said, "I didn't mean that like it sounded. I just want some thinking time right now."

Nathan licked his lips, swallowed hard, then shrugged. "Okay."

"Okay," Ben said, but he knew he had to make some changes in his life. The reactions of Gwen and Nathan proved why. For years he'd kept himself away from people and commitments because in the end somebody always got hurt. He didn't want to be the cause of pain any more than he wanted to be the injured party, and come hell or high water he would make the hard decisions that would get all of them out of this.

He knew it was almost an accident that he'd gotten so involved with Nathan, and he could also see lots of effort and thought would be needed to pull himself away without hurting the boy, but he believed the problems with Gwen were her own doing. He had told her that his involvement in her life was only temporary. He had reminded her constantly that she would soon leave. Because she would. He knew she would. And he was angry with her for making him feel angry with himself for hurting her, when he didn't want to hurt her. Hell, he didn't want to hurt anybody.

When he passed Gwen driving toward town the next

morning, Ben felt a surge of relief, knowing that she was on her way to visit her cousin Hannah, who would take care of her. But immediately following that surge of relief came a rush of guilt. He had told Gwen he would take care of her. He had promised he would be with her, and he felt as if he were deserting her.

Her choice, he reminded himself, and went about his business as usual. Every time a thought of Gwen popped into his brain, he would counter it with the realization that she was safe and sound with her cousin at the day care, surrounded by children and love, exactly where a pregnant woman was supposed to be.

But even as he comforted himself with the knowledge that she was safe, little doubts began to sneak into his musings. Her very presence at the day care would tell the world he was no longer taking care of her, and again, he would look like the bad guy.

Worse, to comfort her, Hannah and Dana might tell her about his past, about how he'd never made a commitment before so they weren't surprised he couldn't make one with Gwen.

He decided it didn't matter. He decided that maybe if Hannah and Dana told her what a washout he was in the love department Gwen would feel that she'd dodged a bullet instead of gotten a broken heart.

Well, that sure as hell didn't cheer him up.

Again, he told himself it didn't matter. His reputation of being a generous but eccentric man got him privacy and peace. And he definitely preferred peace to this gnawing feeling in the pit of his stomach.

But he couldn't seem to stop himself from driving into town at noon. He told himself he only wanted to eat lunch at the diner, but found himself standing in front of Hannah's house, peering into the window, watching Gwen.

Seeing her busy and happy with other people's babies, knowing she was about to have her own baby, only made him feel worse.

If he was worried about having hurt her, seeing her good mood should have brought a burst of relief. Just from the smile on her face, it was easy to see losing him hadn't had the huge impact on her that he had thought it had.

So why the hell did he still feel so damned miserable?

Watching her play with Dana Hewitt's triplets, Ben decided that he felt miserable not because he had hurt her, but because it was *him* who was feeling the loss. She still had her friends. Because of Hannah, she had family. But he had lost the person who was helping him reconnect with his past. He had lost the person he confided in like a best friend. In getting him to commit to be with her until her baby was born, she more or less had promised him at least four weeks of her time. But last night she'd asked him to leave as if the promise had only been one-sided.

But, it hadn't. There were two people in this relationship, not just her. He needed her help. He needed her insight. He couldn't let her emotional highs and lows rule them....

In that second, looking at her joyful face, Ben realized that could be the point. Hormones might have pushed her to say the things she had said last night and she might not have meant a word of it. That was when he finally got the surge of relief, because this explanation made so much sense. Of course, she wasn't upset about the demise of their friendship. She didn't know it was dead. She might have even forgotten all about their argument from the night before. If he walked in right now, she'd probably act as if nothing happened.

And he would get his time back. He wasn't a hundred percent sure what he would do once her baby was born, if he would continue their friendship, waiting for her to leave him, or if the baby would act as a sort of signal that he should leave, but he decided he didn't care. All he knew was that he was incredibly glad that everything was back to normal.

He strolled into the main room of the day care and walked over to where she sat with the triplets.

"Hi."

When she looked up and saw him, her mouth dropped slightly, but she managed a smile, confirming for Ben that things were okay. Back to normal. "Hi."

"I thought I would surprise you and take you to lunch."

She stared at him as if he were crazy.

He scuffed his boot on the rug self-consciously and almost bumped into Dana's little boy. Shifting over a few inches, he said, "It's just that you always cook for me, so I thought I'd return the favor."

"I'm going to have lunch here with the kids," she said slowly, cautiously, then turned her attention to Dana's girls.

Confused, because if she hadn't meant what she had said the night before, she would be nicer to him, Ben said, "Gwen, I want to take you to lunch because I think we need to talk."

"We said everything we needed to say last night."

He almost groaned. He couldn't believe she had meant what she said, but more than that he now understood that he hadn't really responded. Not appropriately, anyway. If he had been wearing his thinking cap, he wouldn't have replied like a man assuming a woman was trapping him. He would have taken her pregnancy into consideration and sidestepped the whole issue. "No, we didn't. Last night everything sort of went crazy. Let's talk today when neither one of us is tired and both of us are thinking straight."

"Is there a problem here?" Hannah asked, palming a mug of coffee as she walked over to where Ben stood towering over Gwen and Dana's triplets.

He never felt so big or so awkward in his entire life and realized why Hannah would be concerned. He swallowed, then tried his most charming smile. "Hi, Hannah. How are you?"

"I'm fine," she said coolly, one eyebrow rising suspiciously. "But I'm not quite sure what you're doing here."

"Trying to talk some sense into your cousin." As he said the words he turned to point at Gwen, only to discover she was gone.

"My cousin is busy," Hannah said. "Because this is a place of business. Since you don't have any children here, I'm afraid I'm going to have to ask you to leave."

He ran his hand along the back of his neck. What in the hell was he doing? Gwen had made it perfectly clear the night before that she didn't want to have anything to do with him. And even if it was only hormones talking, she'd made her bed. He shouldn't care one damned bit to whom she did and didn't talk. Including himself.

"Yeah," he said, then grimaced. "I can see I don't belong here."

Hannah smiled coolly. "Maybe someday."

He glanced around. "I doubt it."

Thinking that Gwen was turning him into a blooming idiot, Ben almost raced to the door. Unfortunately, Dana caught him two seconds before he would have had the knob in his hand. "I know what you're doing," she said.

Angry now, he spun to face her. "Really?" he asked, glaring at her. "That's news to me since I don't even know what in the hell I'm doing myself."

"You think that helping Gwen through this pregnancy is a good thing, but, frankly, Ben, it's the worst thing you can do right now. She's about to have a baby and facing the prospect of being a single mother. Your hurting Gwen was the worst thing that could have happened to her and she's protecting herself...."

"My hurting Gwen?" he asked incredulously. "I didn't hurt her!"

"I don't think you intended to," Dana allowed kindly. "But you did. Which makes it doubly important for you to respect her wishes and stay away from her."

Ben couldn't have agreed more. "Thanks for the advice," he said, then stepped out into the late September morning.

Driving by her house that afternoon, on the way back to his ranch, Ben saw her car, and all the anger he felt while listening to Dana's speech poured through him. Almost as if by automatic pilot, his truck turned into her driveway.

Ben knew that they had to straighten this mess out. He had to. He had finally deduced that whether he wanted to or not, he had hurt her. He hadn't intended to, but he'd seen the signs that she was making more of their relationship than he wanted, and he never stopped her or slowed her down because he was so sure she would get out of the relationship easily after her baby was born. But he hadn't taken her current feelings into consideration, and in fighting his own growing emotions and needs he had confused her. So, technically, he was at fault, and for that reason he had to straighten this mess out.

But more than that, he couldn't stand the fact that she seemed afraid of him at the day care. He genuinely believed knowing that he hadn't intended to hurt her and cared deeply for her would make her feel better.

Rather than walk into her cottage as he normally did, he knocked on her door and then waited for her to answer. When she opened the door and saw it was him, he saw the hope flare in her eyes and it frustrated him. Without any further prompting than that, he said, "Gwen, I did not intend to hurt you."

"I never said you did."

"Obviously, you told your friend Dana that I did," he countered, getting angry again. But he pulled in a silent breath to calm himself. Since Julie, he stayed away from commitments because he didn't want to have this conversation, he didn't want to have this fight. He had not set out to hurt her and she knew that.

"I told you the score up front," he said sadly, because the truth was this hurt him as much as it hurt her. "I don't want to fall in love with you. I don't want to get hurt again by some rich socialite playing house in the country."

Though he expected an outburst of some sort, Ben was surprised when Gwen stuck her nose in the air and marched into her kitchen. "How convenient," she said, walking away from him. "But I'm not buying it. I understand you were hurt by your parents. I understand that you were hurt by your first real love. But I have no intention of hurting you." She turned, then faced him. "I love you. You simply refuse to trust me. I didn't hold the sins of my ex-husband against you and I think it's a cop-out that you hold the sins of your ex-love against me. Since you can't get beyond the past, I don't want to see you again."

Having had no choice but to follow her into her kitchen, Ben stood by her stove. With every sentence she said, his spine stiffened and his brain sharpened. "It's all so easy for you, isn't it? You see everything through rose-colored glasses. But I don't have your happy past. If you can't understand that my past makes it impossible for me to trust, if you can't give me space or time, or even let me have the kind of relationship with you that I want, then you're right. We shouldn't even speak to each other again."

Without waiting for her answer, Ben strode through her kitchen and slammed her front door. Anger flooded through him the whole time he rammed his way to his truck, but when he was seated behind the steering wheel the truth hit him like a tidal wave of emotion. He wasn't angry. He was hurt. He couldn't believe Gwen couldn't see he desperately wanted everything she offered him and it infuriated him to have to face the want day after day, knowing she would take it away the minute she decided she was ready to go back to her own world.

The wound sluiced through him and Ben gritted his teeth against the strength of it. Every cell in his body ached as if with a physical pain, and he wanted to cry out and rail at the world for the injustice of it all, but he refused.

He refused.

As of this moment, he was done suffering over his losses.

Chapter Twelve

But when the phone rang that night at a little after 7 o'clock, Ben grabbed it and said, "Gwen, is everything all right?"

"It's not Gwen," Nina Whitefeather said. "It's Nina, Nathan's foster mother."

Ben scrubbed his hand down his face. "Nina? What's wrong?"

Nina began to cry. "I just got a call from Sheriff Malone. He has Nathan."

"Oh, God," Ben groaned, combing his fingers through his disheveled hair. "What happened?"

"I don't know the details, but the sheriff said something about shoplifting." She paused. "I think it would be better if you would go down to get him."

"So do I," Ben said firmly. "Don't worry, Nina. I'll take care of this."

But though he said "I'll take care of this," when he disconnected the call, he immediately dialed Gwen's number. She answered with a sleepy hello and Ben stopped the surge of confusing emotions that assailed him just from the sound of her voice. They had more important concerns now.

"I just got a call from Nathan's foster mother," he said carefully. "Gwen, don't get all excited, but Nathan's at the sheriff's office."

"Oh, no," Gwen gasped.

"I know," Ben agreed. "All Nina remembered Sheriff Malone saying was something about shoplifting. I think we should go down."

"I think we should, too," Gwen agreed. "You'll stop for me?"

"Be ready in ten minutes."

Gwen dressed quickly and was ready by the time Ben arrived. She didn't wait for him to come into her house, but instead ran out to his truck and managed to get herself in quickly, without his assistance.

"Before you say anything," Ben said, catching her gaze, "I feel guilty enough for both of us. So don't you worry."

"I can't help but worry. For Pete's sake, Ben, we were so involved with ourselves today we didn't even notice that Nathan didn't come around."

He nodded. "I know. We yelled at him for double-dipping, shifted him around while we had our own disagreements, then didn't even notice that he didn't come by today. Some parents we'd make, huh?"

Gwen heard the guilt in his voice, and though she was tempted to shake him for being so thickheaded, she only shook her own head and retreated into her private misery. Not for one minute did she believe she and Ben would make terrible parents. She knew they would make wonderful parents, and so did Nathan.

In fact, that was the problem. And that was why Nathan

avoided them that day. He wanted them to be a family. Given that he was now directing his teachers to contact Gwen rather than Nina, Gwen guessed that in his mind he probably already saw them as a family. But he was also a smart boy, and last night he probably realized Ben was fighting making a commitment to Gwen. And if Ben wouldn't make a commitment to Gwen, then he wasn't committed to the "family." Which meant there was no family and Nathan couldn't deal with that. Worse, when Gwen told Ben not to visit anymore, she also told him not to bring Nathan by either. Ben might have refused to commit, but Gwen was the one who had ended their family.

The truth was Nathan was reaching out for the love and security Gwen was freely offering to Ben, and then watching as Ben handed it back to her.

Saddened by her realizations, Gwen said nothing on the trip. When they parked in front of the sheriff's office, Gwen even got herself out of the truck before Ben could help her. She couldn't believe she was so blind. Here she was giving her love to someone who didn't want it, when all the while there was another person right under her nose who was more than willing to take it.

She allowed Ben to open the door for her, then stepped into the well-lit front room of the sheriff's office. "Hi," Ben said. "We're here for Nathan Eastman."

The dispatcher, Cora Beth Harper, looked up and her brow furrowed. A short, plump woman with black hair, Cora Beth was a fixture in Storkville. Because she was like a mother to everyone, there was genuine concern in her voice when she said, "He's not here. He's too young to be here."

Ben frowned. "But Sheriff Malone called his foster

mother and told her he had Nathan. He said something about shoplifting.''

Then Cora Beth batted her hand. ''Oh, we're not going to bring that sweet baby here!'' she said, incredulous that Ben would think such a thing. ''Sheriff Malone took him over to the day care. Even though it's closed, Nathan would have things to do—books to read and puzzles to play with—so he wouldn't fret the whole time he waited for someone to come get him.''

Gwen sagged with relief and Ben grabbed her arm and directed her out the door. She didn't argue when he helped her into his truck and said nothing as they drove to Hannah's house.

Hannah was waiting at the door. Holding one of her twins in her arms, and carrying the other in a carrier on her back, she said, ''Nathan is going to be so glad to see you.'' She smiled at Gwen and then at Ben. ''And you,'' she added emphatically. ''He's scared to death.''

''What did he do?'' Gwen asked.

''He was with a ring of six teenagers who were picked up for shoplifting,'' Sheriff Tucker Malone said from the entryway to the main room of the day care. A tall man, Sheriff Malone nearly blocked out the light of the brightly lit room behind him. Though he wasn't yet forty, he had silver hair at his temples and the demeanor of a man much wiser than his age. ''Hannah, you got a room we can talk in for some privacy?''

Hannah nodded and pointed to her living room. ''If you guys will keep an eye on the twins, I'll get you coffee.''

Sheriff Malone blew his breath out on a sigh. ''I could certainly use some.''

Hannah walked into the living room ahead of them, and Sheriff Malone directed Gwen and Ben to follow her. ''I'll just put the twins in these baby seats,'' she said, and set the little girl into the seat on the floor in front of the sofa. Then she reached behind her and slid the little boy from his carrier and laid him in the baby seat beside his twin. He immediately grabbed the worn rattle from his sister's chubby fingers and began to play with it. Confused, his sister looked at her empty hand, but rather than cry, she simply stuck her fingers in her mouth and grinned contentedly.

"See, they'll be fine, and I'll only be a minute," Hannah assured everyone before she scurried off.

Wanting to keep a close eye on the babies, Gwen sat on the sofa. Ben took the seat beside her, and Sheriff Malone sat in the big chair across from them.

"Here's what I've pieced together must have happened. For weeks, the store manager had been watching a group of teens who were coming into his shop, spending a lot of time and not really buying much of anything. Maybe a pack of gum or a candy bar here and there, but nothing that would warrant the amount of time they spent in the store."

"So he figured they weren't paying for the things they had picked up in the back aisles," Ben suggested when Tucker drew a breath.

"That's about the size of it," Tucker agreed. "The thing is he hasn't seen Nathan with the group before today."

"He's usually with me," Gwen agreed hurriedly. "He couldn't possibly be a part of the group."

"That might be true," Tucker said. "But he was with them today, and he had things in his jacket."

"Oh, for God's sake, Tucker, he's nine," Ben said. "And this is his first offense."

"Precisely. I don't want to make a repeat offender out of him. That's why he's here instead of in jail. This little boy doesn't belong with these kids. I don't know why he was with them. And all the store owner and I need is some assurance that he won't ever be with them again and we're willing to let him go with a stern warning."

Ben knew Sheriff Malone was waiting for something from them, a commitment of sorts. From her behavior over the past few days, he also knew Gwen couldn't make that commitment. So what Tucker Malone wanted was a commitment from Ben, a promise that he would watch over Nathan.

Hannah entered the living room, a tray in her hands and Nathan on her heels. The minute Gwen saw him, she bounced off the couch and ran to him.

"Oh, Nathan," she cried, hugging the little boy to her with a sob. "I am so sorry," she said, and began to cry in earnest.

Nathan cried right with her. "I'm sorry, too, Gwen," he said. "I was so scared. They told me if I didn't take something they would hit me."

"Who would hit you?" Gwen demanded, pushing Nathan far enough away that she could look into his eyes.

"The bigger boys," Nathan admitted quietly. Then he caught her gaze. "I know that's not an excuse," he began, but his lips trembled and he began to sob again.

But as concerned as he was with Nathan, Ben felt an even greater stab of panic about Gwen when she sagged tiredly. To Ben she looked weak enough to faint. Instead, with a little help from Sheriff Malone, she managed to get to her feet and direct Nathan to the sofa, where she sat beside him.

"Oh, Nathan, I'm sorry you got into this mess, because it's my fault," she said, putting her arms around the sobbing child, who nestled into her side.

Watching them, Ben swallowed, suddenly seeing he

was wrong about Gwen making a commitment to Nathan. She might have been cautious about going too far too fast with Nathan, but now that the chips were down, it was easy to see she was definitely in his corner. She was tired and alone. Nathan was frightened and alone. But just from the way she was behaving, Ben could tell she had every intention of taking care of both of them. Whether it was here in Storkville, or thousands of miles away with her family, Gwen would mother Nathan. And no matter what problem or difficulty confronted them, Gwen would handle it.

Ben also realized that she could do that, and she would do it alone. He could walk out of their lives and Gwen and Nathan would get along without him. He didn't need to make any commitments to Nathan. He didn't need to make any commitments to Gwen. They didn't need him.

That wounded his pride, of course, but worse, Ben relived flashes of memory of himself with Nathan over the past year and with Gwen over the past few weeks and he felt a huge hole form in his heart. If he walked away right now, they would be fine, but he wouldn't. Nathan might not be his blood child, but in Ben's heart, Nathan was his son.

And Gwen was his woman.

Watching Gwen soothe and cuddle the boy, Ben knew in his heart that these people were his. His to watch. His to protect. And his to enjoy. Whether he and Gwen had intended to or not, they had formed a family. And no matter where they went, they would always be a family. Time and place didn't matter—didn't mean anything. Bonds did. Love did. Love didn't exactly "conquer" all, but it was the glue he had been missing in his other relationships. With Gwen he had the love that would keep them together no matter where they lived, or how they lived.

And this was the piece of information for which he had always been searching. This was the final piece of his life puzzle. He didn't need to live in a certain place, or behave a certain way, he needed people to love, people to commit to, and he had found them.

Before Ben could pull himself out of his thoughts, Sheriff Malone approached him. "I don't see any reason to press charges against Nathan," he whispered. "From what I just overheard it almost sounds like the older boys threatened to hurt Nathan if he didn't go along. I can't punish him for that."

Ben agreed. "And it appears Nathan has learned his lesson."

Sheriff Malone glanced at Nathan, then back at Ben. "I think you're right. But I also think you should take him home for the night. And that maybe you and Mrs. Parker should make out an official schedule of times each of you will be responsible for him to make sure Nathan doesn't accidentally get into a situation like this again," Tucker said, confirming again that he wanted a commitment from either Ben or Gwen or both of them. "He's a high-spirited boy," the sheriff continued, again glancing at Nathan. "And his foster parents might be finding him a little too much to handle. Nathan appears to have taken a liking to you and Gwen and he listens to you. With a little thought, I'm sure you and Gwen could work out a plan to mentor Nathan through life and keep him out of trouble."

Because Ben had been watching Gwen as Tucker spoke, he smiled. While Sheriff Malone was telling Ben that he and Gwen needed to take charge of Nathan, Gwen was telling Nathan that she could never be happy without him in her life, affirming that she also saw the bond they had formed. Ben didn't have to explain it to her because she saw it. Maybe she had always seen it.

Suddenly, clearly, he realized that if he wanted it, everything he needed could be falling into place right now. All he had to do was reach out and take it.

"Oh, my gosh," Sheriff Malone said suddenly. "Would you look at this?"

Pulled out of his reverie, Ben said, "What? I'm sorry. What did you say?"

"Look at this rattle."

Hannah raced over. "What?" Closely examining the rattle in the bright light of the lamp beside the sofa as Sheriff Malone had, Ben recognized Hannah obviously saw what the sheriff had seen. "What is that?" she asked curiously.

"It's the McCormack family crest," Tucker said incredulously. "Well, I'll be damned. Looks like these kids have a connection to Storkville after all."

While Hannah and Sheriff Malone studied the rattle and Hannah quietly speculated that this could mean Quentin McCormack was the twins' father, Ben watched Gwen. Nathan was quiet now, not crying anymore, and, though tired, Gwen looked about as relieved and content as a person could look. Awestruck, Ben stood frozen. He had a family. He almost couldn't believe it, but there they were, right before his eyes. In little over a month, he had been handed the gift for which he had been searching for decades.

Numb, but more certain of this than anything before, Ben said, "Gwen, could I see you in the playroom for a second?"

She glanced down at Nathan, then back at Ben, and it appeared she might refuse him if only because Nathan was clinging to her, but Hannah said, "Hey, Nate, let's get you a cup of cocoa before you have to go. That way you'll be warm all the way home."

Nathan peered at Gwen, Gwen nodded her approval, and Nathan allowed Hannah to escort him into the kitchen.

Because Sheriff Malone was making notes in a small book he'd pulled from his shirt pocket, Ben hustled Gwen into the activity room of the day care.

Without explanation or preamble, he took her by the shoulders and looked into her eyes. "Did you mean what you said to Nathan? That you could never be happy without him in your life?"

Straightening her spine, Gwen said, "I most certainly did." Holding his gaze, she added, "I'm thinking about adopting him."

Ben was so relieved he could have collapsed. Amazed, overjoyed, he pulled Gwen into his arms. "Good, because I want to adopt Nathan, too."

Flustered because she didn't want Ben cuddling up to her and then leaving her again, Gwen pushed out of his arms. "I'll fight you to the bitter end for Nathan's custody."

But Ben only laughed. "Darling, you won't have to fight me at all if we adopt him together."

Now her eyes narrowed. The use of the endearment hadn't escaped her notice, but if anything it infuriated her. She wanted nothing but the best for Nathan and a male role model who flitted into and out of their lives was not the best. "I don't see how we'll do that...."

"You'll marry me."

"I'm not..." she began, but when what he said sunk in, she backed away. "I'll what?"

"Marry me," he said simply, happily. He pressed his

palms to both her cheeks and kissed her soundly. "I love you. I love you," he said again, and the words wove through her like music on the wind. "I love the family we've made together and I want it to last forever. *This* is what I've been searching for all my life. And when I finally found it I was so consumed by the unusual circumstances of my life that I almost didn't see it. What I wanted was the most simple, most basic thing of all. Just love, acceptance… Day-to-day stuff."

Shocked, Gwen couldn't even speak. Finally she managed to reply, "I don't know what to say."

"Say you will marry me and that we'll adopt Nathan, and then you will let me adopt your child, too."

Astounded now, Gwen took another pace back, and Ben hauled her into his arms again. "I'm not kidding. What I was was blinded by too much information."

She peered at him skeptically.

"All right," he admitted sheepishly. "Maybe I was also foolish and stupid and scared," he said, holding her tightly. "But you've known that all along, haven't you?"

She nodded.

"You don't have to be so annoyingly right about it."

Gwen couldn't help it, she laughed. "You're just mad because my instincts about us make me look smarter than you."

"You're not smarter than me."

"Of course I am," she said sweetly, then kissed him. "But you're stronger and in general you have more integrity, so I need to keep you around to help Nathan."

"And the little one?" Ben asked, placing his palm atop Gwen's tummy.

Tears filled Gwen's eyes and she licked her suddenly dry lips. It was easy to tease and laugh about their commitment; in some ways she also believed it was the right thing to do. She, Ben and Nathan had all had enough tears and sadness in their lives. But right now, right at this minute, it was more than appropriate to be serious.

She drew a long breath and looked up into Ben's dark eyes. "And the little one," she whispered. "I can't think of a better father for my baby, because there isn't anyone in this world I love as much as I love you."

As if absorbing that, Ben closed his eyes and was silent for a few seconds, then he dropped a quick kiss on her lips and turned her toward the playroom door. "Let's go get our son."

* * * * *

Chapter One

He'd been slimed!

Quentin McCormack looked down and watched cotton candy, Hawaiian punch and chocolate mix together and slide down his leg. The triple whammy.

Then he met the worried, gray-eyed gaze of the pint-size linebacker who'd collided with him. Contrition was written all over his face, and Quentin hadn't the heart to reprimand the little guy even though the trousers were new and expensive. He also hadn't a clue how old the boy was, but he was definitely too little to be wandering around alone.

"You okay, buddy?" he asked.

The boy, who barely came up to Quentin's knee, nodded tentatively.

"Where's your mom and dad?"

His only response was a shrug. Quentin surveyed the lunchtime crowd. It was August and hot. Hannah Brady had just cut the ribbon to open her new day-care center. Most everyone in town was there for the ceremony because Storkville took its responsibility to children very seriously. Which made him wonder who would let their child wander unattended.

Just then he heard a panic-tinged female voice calling out. He looked down at the child. "What's your name?"

"Wookie," he answered.

"Like the Star Wars character?" he asked. He wouldn't be surprised. For all he knew the boy was speaking an alien language.

The crowd parted and two feet from him, Quentin saw a frantic-looking woman holding the hands of two little girls with tear-streaked faces. His breath caught as he stared at her. Shoulder-length, chestnut-brown curls framed a heart-shaped face with the biggest, most expressive gray eyes he'd ever seen. She wasn't tall, maybe five foot two, but her slender body, with curves in all the right places, was his fantasy come to life.

Lightning.

A direct hit. He couldn't have felt more zapped if he'd been standing in an electrical storm holding a kite string with a key attached.

Because of the crowd on blocked-off Main Street, she didn't notice him or his new little friend. To get the woman's attention, he held up his hand, then curled his fingers into his palm when he noticed it was shaking. She finally looked directly at him and he pointed down.

"Is he by any chance yours?"

Bingo, he thought when her shoulders drooped with relief. She was beside him in three strides and squatted down on a level with the child.

"Lukie, you scared me half to death," she said in a voice that was three parts concern and one part anger. Then she pulled him into her arms for a viselike hug. "Don't *ever* run off like that again, young man."

"His name isn't Wookie?" Quentin asked.

She stood and smiled, taking his breath away for the second time in two minutes. "His name is Lukas, and articulating *L*s is a challenge for a three-year-old."

"Hewwo, Mommy," the child said, his red-stained mouth turning up in a grin.

"Hi, Lukie." She looked back at Quentin and shrugged. "See what I mean? His sisters have the same problem."

"They're *all* three?" he asked, surveying the children who were about the same size. Stunned, he watched her nod. "You must be from Storkville," he said, shaking his head.

"You mean because the stork who visits Storkville bestows many bouncing bundles on those whose love is boundless?" she asked, her gray eyes twinkling.

"That's the legend," he concurred.

"I think the stork had a navigational malfunction that day because he visited me in Omaha. And—" she glanced at the three children with infinite love "—I don't know if he bestowed bouncing bundles as much as the triple whammy."

"My exact thought," he said, remembering his close encounter of the gooey kind. "But not about children. Cotton candy, Hawaiian punch and chocolate is an awful lot of junk food for a little guy like this," Quentin commented. "Not to mention the fact that he's running around unsupervised, Mrs.—"

"Dana Hewitt," she said, introducing herself. "I'm aware that a three-year-old needs supervision, Mr.—"

"McCormack. Quentin McCormack."

"Do you have children, Mr. McCormack?" she asked.

"I'm not married," he said.

"That's not what I asked. Your marital status doesn't preclude fathering children."

"For me it does. I would never be that irresponsible," he said, meeting her gaze.

"Have you ever heard the saying 'Never judge a man—or woman—until you've walked in their shoes'?"

"Yes."

"Good. Here's another one. When you have triplets, we'll talk." She reclaimed the hands of her two still-sniffling girls. "Not that it's any of your business, but each of the children was allowed to choose one treat. While I was paying for them, Lukie grabbed his and the girls', too, and took off while my back was turned."

"I see. I didn't mean to judge. You're right. I haven't a clue how to deal with one child, let alone three the same age. Sorry."

"Apology accepted," she said. When she looked at her son, her anger faded and a different sort of mad-tender look suffused her features. "You are in a lot of trouble, young man. Taking your sisters' treats…" Dana heaved an exasperated sigh and shook her head at her son. "Give Molly back her cotton candy and Kelly her chocolate." She looked closer and for the first time seemed to notice his empty hands. "You couldn't have eaten all of that so fast."

Quentin saw the exact moment when she started to put together what happened. Her gaze went to her son's sticky, empty hands, then the circle of goo surrounding his own Italian leather loafers, finally up to his designer pant legs that were now so stiff they could stand up by themselves.

Her eyes and mouth opened wide and rounded into O's. "Good heavens," she said. "And if there's a God residing there, *my* son didn't do that to you."

"Don't worry about it. Accidents happen."

"Oh, Lukie, tell Mr. McCormack sorry."

The boy looked up at him. "Sorry, Mr. Mac."

"It's okay, pal," he said, ruffling the boy's hair.

"It's Mr. McCormack," she corrected her son.

"That's a pretty big mouthful," he said. "Mac's fine."

"I can't tell you how sorry I am about this Mr. Mc—"

"Please call me Quentin."

"All right, Quentin," she said. "I insist you let me have your trousers cleaned for you."

"That's a tough one. Unless you want me to drop 'em right here in front of God and everyone on Main Street."

She blushed and the look went straight to his heart, infiltrating his defenses without firing a shot. Of course it didn't hurt that she had a sweet smile, with full, sensuous lips, and curls around her face that looked as if a man had run his hands through her hair while kissing her senseless. The combination was his second triple whammy in the last five minutes....

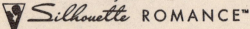

**Don't miss
an exciting opportunity
to save on the purchase of
Harlequin and Silhouette books!**

Buy any two Harlequin or
Silhouette books and save
$10.00 off future Harlequin
and Silhouette purchases

OR

buy any three
Harlequin or Silhouette books
and save **$20.00 off** future
Harlequin and Silhouette purchases.

*Watch for details
coming in October 2000!*

PHQ400

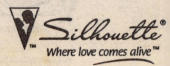

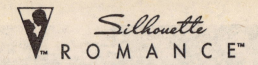

COMING NEXT MONTH